THE VANISHING PATIENT

A DR CATHY MORELAND MYSTERY #BOOK SEVEN

MAIRI CHONG

BLOODHOUND
— BOOKS —

ALSO BY MAIRI CHONG

For W – every one has been and every one will always be.

1

There were three of them by the graveside, but not one of them mourned. At the head of the grave stood the minister. He was in his late sixties and weather-beaten from decades of service. The elderly man shifted and cleared his throat but there was little to say. Although he knew that what they were doing was surely unethical, he had not asked questions.

The cemetery was newish, sited high up on the outskirts of the town. Some of the locals had complained about the necessity to erect one. It wasn't like the old days when every Scottish family bought a plot, choosing their final resting place beside a long line of forefathers. People were done with those kinds of traditions now. They wanted a cheap, clean funeral. They no longer sought solace in religion at all.

But the small, grey church with its graveyard was there, all the same. It was secluded as was necessary, with high metal gates. There were no houses within sight and few walked up this far, especially when the nights were drawing in. Below them, the lines of orange street lamps lit the roadsides. Car headlights moved in a convoluted serpent as commuters made their way home to warm kitchens and eager loved ones, unaware of the solemn proceedings close by.

It was almost dusk and a thin drizzle hung in the air. It had been threatening to rain all day. Not heavy enough to warrant an overcoat, but just sufficient to thoroughly chill the suited men. They stood now, heads bowed and shoulders hunched until the minister was done with his obligatory words. One of the men coughed and rubbed his neck. His colleague glanced sideways, momentarily studying the other's face. Neither spoke.

The edges of the grave had not been covered with the customary green cloth as would have been usual for a burial. Instead, due to the haste of the arrangements, the grave had been dug that evening by the sexton. The sides of the earth were sharp and damp, cut deep into the red-brown clay of the land. The mechanical digger rested nearby, an irreverent and garish bystander. The coffin bore no name and only a simple, square headstone would mark it eventually. The inscription would be vague.

Afterwards, they didn't linger. One of the suited men shook the minister's hand. They made their way back to their black saloon. The minister watched as the car pulled out of the cemetery and onto the glistening tarmac. The wheels swished. He stood and listened to the drone of the car engine until it joined the chorus of the other cars far below. Slowly, he made his way back to the church.

2

'Missing?' Dr Cathy Moreland asked, leaning forward in her chair and looking intently at the patient before her. 'How do you mean missing?'

A strand of dark hair fell across her cheek and she tucked it behind her ear. Her room had been cold coming in that morning and despite the radiator behind her being turned up full, she still found herself pulling the loose folds of her cardigan about her. She had hoped that this might be a straightforward consultation. A chance to catch up. She was already running behind.

The man before her bristled. 'Well, just what I say,' he replied. 'I don't expect you to do anything about it, of course. I've already spoken to the police. Not that they were interested. They assumed it was some kind of domestic fallout.' The man's upper lip twitched in disgust. 'No,' he said vehemently. 'But I do want to put in an official complaint about the bloody doctor who came out last night. Damn cheek it was, and I'm sure it was him that locked me in my bedroom.'

Dr Moreland blinked a couple of times trying to process this statement.

The man, named Adam Steer, wasn't especially known to the surgery. He was in his late-fifties and rather comfortably off, as far as she could establish. His clothes were casual but expensive-looking, and he had kept himself in reasonable shape. Dr Moreland had glanced at his notes just prior to him coming in, as she often did before greeting a patient. Twice in the past five years, he had attended with mild anxiety due to uncertainties at work, and once he had come in with an uncomplicated upper respiratory tract infection. On each occasion, he had been given verbal advice only.

Dr Moreland smiled and her brow wrinkled in an attempt to look empathetic despite the man's tone. 'Tell me about it, Mr Steer,' she said. Although her interest had been piqued, her voice was level as if the words had been spoken many times before. She was rarely shocked by anything she heard these days. 'I'm not sure I understand you,' she admitted. 'Your wife? She's disappeared after a doctor visit?'

'Yes,' he said slapping the palm of his hand down on her desk and making her flinch. 'Last night.'

Cathy had been a partner at the Glainkirk Practice for seven years and was not used to such unexpected outbursts, especially during a routine Tuesday morning surgery. She looked down at the polished desk. The man removed his hand from the surface. Her eyes fixed on the damp imprint left behind. Cathy forced her attention back to his face. His forehead was heavy and his brows, had they not been diligently groomed would have undoubtedly met in a thick streak. 'I can see that you're upset, Mr Steer. Please, if I can help, I will. Explain to me what happened last night. Take your time. I do want to help you.'

Finally, this seemed to break the man's audacity. He lapsed back in his chair and for the first time, Cathy noted the dark shadows beneath his eyes, only accentuated by the strip light above her desk. He ran his hands back and forth on the knees to his trousers as he spoke.

'Oh God, what a night!' he said with feeling. 'I don't know where to begin. We'd been in India these last few months. Business. Not a big success, I'll admit,' he said, shaking his head. 'I'd come back home before her. I was to get the house ready and she was to follow on. She returned last week. Hardly been out since. Said she had a cold. More like a bad flu, I thought. My God, it seems like a lifetime ago.'

Cathy waited. She noted the thin line of perspiration on his top lip. He wiped this with his forefinger and thumb and the skin rasped.

'Well, she wasn't herself,' he continued. 'That, I knew. It was as if she wasn't even glad to be home. Moped around for days. Then came down with this cold, so she said. I told her it was to be expected what with sitting on a plane for seven hours with a hundred other people's germs only last week. I thought nothing more of it until later on.' His eyes flicked over Cathy as if assessing her response. His lips were thin and he licked the lower, moistening it for a moment before it once more looked cracked and dry. 'I offered to get her a hot honey and lemon, all the usual stuff. She didn't want to make a fuss though. She was short with me. Said that she just needed her bed.'

'What was wrong? You say a cold, but was it a headache? A runny nose?'

'A headache, yes. She kept rubbing at her temples, and she was flushed. Her face looked red. I told her to go upstairs. I said I'd check on her later. Bring her paracetamol and a little something to eat.'

'But she got worse? You said you had called the out-of-hours doctor? When was that?'

'Much later. She'd settled, you see? She seemed quite herself again. My brother came past the house to ask about the trip. I hadn't managed to speak with him since we returned. It's a family business,' Mr Steer explained. 'He said he'd wanted to check we'd both arrived back safely. We spoke for a while but Marjorie didn't come down. I was sleeping in the spare bedroom that night.' He suddenly looked self-conscious. 'To give her the bed to herself what with feeling unwell. After my brother left, I popped my head around the door to check before I turned in myself and she was sitting up writing in her diary and said that she must have had a migraine, but it had passed. I fetched her a glass of water to have by the bed overnight and said goodnight.'

'So, what had happened to warrant the doctor call-out?'

'Damn man he was when he did come,' Mr Steer ejected savagely. 'Looked smart enough at first glance, but was way out of his depth and didn't listen to a thing I said.'

Dr Moreland's eyebrows arched, but she didn't speak.

'Worse. She got much worse,' he said testily. 'I woke up at just after eleven. We'd turned in early. I'd been bloody exhausted, still jet-lagged. I took paracetamol myself. My throat was sore and I started to imagine I was getting a fever. Maybe it was just in my head what with her being the same. Anyway, I read for a short while after I'd been in to see her. Her room was quiet so I assumed she'd managed to get some rest. The best thing for her, I thought. I must have turned my light out at about ten. I fell asleep almost right away, but a noise woke me. I sat up in bed with such a start. I barely knew where I was at first, but then I heard her in the next room moving about and I looked at the clock. It was just gone eleven so we'd not been asleep long at all. I went through, of course. I was concerned she'd become unwell again.'

'And?' Cathy had already begun to wonder if the man's wife had contracted malaria. It seemed plausible given her recent foreign travel and the symptoms that he'd already described.

'Oh God! She was much worse. It was like she was delirious.

She was pacing up and down and shivering. When I touched her, her skin was roasting. Her nightdress was damp with sweat.'

This seemed only to confirm Cathy's suspicions. 'So, you called the out-of-hours doctors then? That was wise.'

'Of course,' he said. 'Although my bloody phone went missing and I had to jog up to my brother's and get him to call. He wasn't best pleased about being woken himself, but he could see I was in a state. There's no line into the house, we have to use our mobiles,' he explained. 'My brother told me to go back and wait. He'd sort it out and he said I looked dreadful too. I felt it. The doctor came within ten or fifteen minutes. Very fast. I'd been in a panic and he must have realised it was urgent. It surprised me though, how quickly he came, but as soon as I saw him, I knew I'd made a mistake. I should've just told my brother to ring for an ambulance and been done with it.'

'What did the doctor think?'

'He messed around. He had a funny sort of a doctors' bag. More of a rucksack. He spent an age, taking down notes. Shone a torch in her mouth and checked her temperature, but didn't listen to her chest. He barely laid a hand on her. Did most of his consultation from the end of the bloody bed. I pulled him up on it as it happens. Asked him if he didn't want to examine her properly. He smirked at that, the damn cheek, and said that he was fairly certain of the diagnosis. Said that it might well be meningitis. That made me panic even more. She'd had that headache I suppose, and she was rubbing her back a bit. I asked why she didn't have a rash. I always thought people with meningitis had that, but he said it was often the much more advanced cases that had the rash.'

Cathy raised her eyebrows once more. Meningitis wasn't outwith the possible differential diagnoses she supposed, but it didn't quite fit.

'He was rummaging in his bag again,' the man continued.

'Said he had some tablets he wanted to give her. Asked me to go downstairs and get her a glass of water and to run her a cold bath.'

Cathy was, quite frankly, astounded by this and struggled to conceal the fact. There were, admittedly, two types of meningitis: bacterial and viral. The viral strain was undoubtedly less severe, but if the doctor had had any doubt, he would surely have admitted her for observation at the very least. Either way, it was certainly not the expected procedure. Had she seen a similar case and thought meningitis was a possibility, she would have immediately administered an intramuscular injection of penicillin. She carried a vial in her doctors' bag always. Then she would have phoned for an ambulance straight away. Oral medication of any sort would be useless and as for running a cold bath, well, it wasn't in any part of the treatment guidelines. Not wanting to worry the man further by casting doubt on the other doctor's care, she nodded. 'What happened then?'

'Well, I did what the blasted man asked. I was properly spooked by that point, and Marjorie was utterly exhausted and barely able to hold herself upright. I went into the spare room where I'd been sleeping myself before all the hullabaloo. It has an en suite, and I took the empty glass that had been by her bedside. She must have drank it all already due to the fever that night. I ran the cold tap for a while and filled the glass, and I began running a bath. Not completely cold though. I ran some hot in too, so she didn't startle getting in. It could only have been a couple of minutes. I let the bath continue running and went back through with the glass of water, thinking that the doctor would want it so she could take the tablets he had. I was sure I hadn't closed the bedroom door behind me, but when I turned around, it was shut. I tried the handle and the bloody thing was locked.'

'Surely not. It was just that the door had jammed behind you.'

The man shook his head fiercely. 'Explain to me this then,' he said. 'Why, when I put my shoulder to it, did it not budge? I hammered on that damn door and called out. Admittedly, I could understand that my wife was too unwell to come, but the blasted doctor. He could have opened it.'

Cathy was at a loss. 'So...' she began, but tailed off, not knowing quite what to say.

'So, I was furious, as you might imagine. I stopped running the bath. Then I hollered and thumped at the door. No one came. I must have been stuck for a good fifteen or twenty minutes until I managed to force my way out, and by that time, they were gone.'

'What? The doctor disappeared with your wife?'

'I've no idea if they left as a pair. I can only suppose so. At the time, I assumed he must have taken her directly to the hospital and it had all been a mistake, the whole thing. Maybe I'd misunderstood his instructions about the bath or something. Anyway, I went over to my brother's again and phoned of course. I spent half an hour ringing around, but there was nothing. No one had heard of a Marjorie Steer being admitted. I gave up after I'd called the two main hospitals. I spoke to A&E and to the main switchboards that covered the wards. Nothing. I paced about a bit and thought about heading out myself to look for some sign of them. By then, it was gone two in the morning. I didn't know what to think. I sat up all night and waited, hoping that I'd get a call to explain what had happened, but nothing. When it came to six o'clock, I knew something dreadful had occurred. That was when I reported it to the police.'

'It certainly seems very odd. But you said at the start that the police weren't concerned? What did they think then?'

'They asked a lot of impertinent questions about the state of our marriage and then they looked in her diary.' His face grew an even deeper red than it had become in the storytelling. 'It was practically the first thing they did when they went up to the bedroom. She'd written some nonsense about wanting to leave me. It must have been delirium though. I told them that there was nothing wrong. That was part of the reason we'd gone abroad in the first place, to start afresh. Admittedly, the thing hadn't panned out as it should, but we were fine. Marjorie and I were back on track. There'd been no talk of... well, no one had been mentioned while we were away, at all. It was in the past. I forgave her for that and we moved on.'

Cathy looked questioningly at Mr Steer.

'A friendship,' he said petulantly. 'Before our trip. I'd not approved. I'd been working too many long hours.'

'So, the police thought the whole thing was simply a trick; the whole illness? So that she could go. But why? Why not just leave? And what about the doctor?'

'Exactly,' he said, once again hitting his hand down on the desk. 'Not to mention that she left in her nightdress and slippers, taking nothing with her. I went over every inch of her room that night as I waited. I know she didn't take anything else. Even her handbag was still there, with her purse and passport, so the police were wrong. Disappeared into thin air.' Mr Steer suddenly seemed to grow tired of all the questions. 'I'll not trouble you any further. I can see you're busy,' he said. He was keen to conclude things and Cathy felt that thus far, she had been of little help. 'All I want is to see the doctor who was on-call last night. When I find him, I'll get to the bottom of this damn business,' Mr Steer said.

'What was his name?' she asked. 'All the surrounding doctors' practices cover this area out of hours. We take it in turns. I'm sure we can find out what happened.'

'Well, he said he was from here. That's why I came. He didn't say much but he told me that. Said he was from this practice. Gave the name of Dr Hope.'

Cathy inhaled sharply. Of all the things the man had said to her, despite their sensational nature, this was by far the most shocking. 'There must have been a misunderstanding.'

'I'm not mistaken. That's exactly what he told me,' he replied obstinately. 'If you're trying to protect a colleague, you can forget it. I need to get to the bottom of this. I need to find my wife.'

Cathy was silent for a moment or two. Her hands shook and she felt suddenly sick. When she spoke, her voice jarred. 'I'm afraid there must have been a misunderstanding, Mr Steer. Dr Hope didn't come to your house last night. He died three years ago.' Cathy swallowed. 'He was murdered in this practice.'

3

About eleven o'clock of the same morning, and a good half-hour late in finishing her surgery, Cathy sat before her computer and considered. There were house-calls to attend to but she remained seated, staring blankly at the flickering screen. Her leg bobbed back and forth and she chewed the edges of a fingernail. The encounter had troubled her a good deal. What on earth had the man meant? Was it possible that the entire story was a farce, and of whose making, his, or his wife's? If it was true, and she was doubtful, then did that mean that they had someone in their midst impersonating a doctor? And not just any doctor, but her dead practice partner. The entire thing seemed too outrageous.

Cathy sighed and, tired of the blank computer screen in front of her, instead turned her gaze out of the window. Her room looked onto the practice car park. She watched a patient's car reversing. Due to the dullness of the day, its lights were on half-beam and caught at her window momentarily, illuminating the already stark walls. Since she had qualified as a GP principal, Cathy's time had been tumultuous, to say the least. Quite apart from her distressing personal circumstances, due to which she was regularly seeing her own GP as a matter of routine, there had been so many changes. Since Dr Hope's death some three and a half years ago, the practice had altered a good deal. They now had a new practice manager, a new practice partner just these last few months, and then, only last week, James, her senior partner, had announced that he was planning to retire in the spring. Change was always difficult, but it seemed that they had experienced more than their fair share recently.

Cathy swallowed. Her throat felt dry. She traced the line of her jaw and along the sides of her neck, feeling for the submandibular glands. She found that they were painful to touch. She was undoubtedly coming down with something. A hot drink would help. It was nearly coffee-time but she should be getting on. In the room next to her, James would be finishing his morning surgery. She heard the scrape of a chair moving and the flick of a light switch. Getting up, she walked to her door that Mr Steer had slammed as he had left. Opening it now, she came face-to-face with James.

The man, although nearing the finish of his career as a general practitioner, was still as affable as probably he had been at the beginning. He certainly hadn't lost his love for the job, and since his wife's death some eight years ago, he had thrown himself into the work, perhaps taking on more than his more junior staff. Taller than Cathy, and stooping ever so slightly, he smiled gently at her. The lines around his eyes had undeniably increased in number since she had begun working with him but he was still a handsome man.

'Oh, Cathy,' he said, adjusting his doctors' bag and a set of notes under his arm. 'I'm just heading off. A bad one was it?'

She smiled. 'Thanks for your help. I had noticed you saw a couple from my list. I'll return the favour sometime, but you never seem to run late.' She had seen on the computer screen that her partner had taken in two patients who had been booked in to see her that morning, obviously realising that she was running behind. 'Neither needed to see me in particular, did they, James?' she checked.

The elderly doctor shook his head. 'No. Just one-offs and easily sorted. I see Euan's put his name down for three visits already. Have you got many to do?'

'Just Mrs Carney, and the Earles. I could put them off until later in the week, but it'll only mount up.'

The man began to pass her in the corridor, moving towards the fire exit that they all used rather than leaving through the main reception.

'James?' she said, and he turned, perhaps hearing the note of concern in her voice. 'I've just had an odd one. Have you got a second?' Cathy knew that it would help to talk, and of all people, James was invariably the first she would go to with a problem. 'You don't know anything about a couple called Steer, do you? Married and living on the Ancrum Road I think? They've just returned from India apparently. I've had him in this morning with a very strange story of his wife going missing.' Cathy paused before going on. Her senior partner tilted his head to one side. 'He said a man claiming that he was an out-of-hours GP came to their house last night, but that the doctor's etiquette was highly questionable. James, I don't know what to think.'

James raised his thinning eyebrows. 'I'm intrigued now, Cathy.' He smiled. 'What's it all about?'

'Well, it only gets worse. Mr Steer said that this man, the one who declared himself to be a doctor, locked him in his spare room, and when Mr Steer did manage to get out, the doctor had disappeared along with his wife! I know. It's utterly ludicrous, isn't it?'

'Does Mr Steer have a history of mental health issues, by any chance?' James asked.

'That's just it,' Cathy said. 'Nothing major at all. A bit of mild anxiety. I think it was you who saw him a good five years back the first time, and then I'd had him in a year or so ago, not that I can remember. He's a funny man. Well-to-do. A bit full of himself, I suppose. I have to say that if he was delusional, he came across as very plausible.'

'What made him come in today? Surely it was a police matter if he thought his wife had been spirited away.'

'Well, that's true of course. It gets even crazier. He said that the doctor who attended had said he was from our practice. That's why he'd come to us this morning. He came in, all guns blazing, ready for a row. Wanted to know who the man was and what he'd done with his wife.'

James snorted. 'Oh yes? Which one of us was it then? Me? Euan? You're out of the frame along with Linda, I assume, being female.'

'James,' Cathy said, now quite serious. 'He said that the man had called himself Dr Hope. I know,' she continued, in response to his look. 'It's horrible, isn't it?'

'Well,' said James, finally. 'He's rattled you. It does sound to me as if it needs looking into. How have you left it with him?'

'He said that he'd called the police already but they weren't overly interested. They think his wife's run off and left him. Reading between the lines, it sounds as if they've been having some marital difficulties.'

'Is he coming back to see you? I'm just thinking about risk to himself or others.'

'I know.' Cathy sighed. 'I was a bit taken aback and I don't think I handled it very well. I should have firmed up a return appointment. He was so full of bluster that it was difficult to negotiate with him. At the time, I was in shock because of him mentioning Mark's name. I don't think he's a major risk. You think he's psychotic, I suppose?'

The other doctor shook his head. 'I'm not saying that but it's a bit strange. Have you looked at the wife's notes, out of interest? Any family nearby who might be able to shed some light on it?'

'I was going to look. I just heard you going out and wanted to run it by you.'

He nodded. 'Do a quick check, Cathy, even if it's just to settle your mind. Listen, I'd better head. One of my visits is a query urinary retention. We'll catch up later, all right? I'll be interested to hear what else you manage to unearth.'

'I should get on myself, but I'm worrying now.'

'Put off the Earles and the other one until later if they're not urgent. I'll be back in an hour or so, and you can fill me in. I'm sure there'll be an explanation.'

Cathy smiled grimly as he left. If there was a good explanation, she'd love to hear it. Returning to her room she made a couple of phone calls. The Earles would be in that afternoon and she arranged to pop in on her way home after evening surgery. Mrs Carney said that the medication was already working wonders and she would see the doctor later in the week. Absolved of her obligations, Cathy logged in to the computer system once again, and typed in the name 'Steer.'

When James returned from his visits, he found Cathy still in her room.

'Well?' he asked. 'What news?'

Cathy smiled. 'It only gets stranger, if that's possible.'

James came in and shut the door. 'Come on then. I was barely able to think of anything else when I was out. It's a proper mystery.'

'So, I looked,' she said. 'It's just the two of them on our books, as far as I can see, and no mention of children or close family, although he did mention a brother. I assume the brother's registered with the Westfield Practice and not us. I checked out Mrs Steer's records as you suggested. If anything, it's worried me more. Linda apparently saw her on a couple of occasions as it happens, before they went to India. It seems that the marital difficulties were somewhat more extreme than I had previously understood. Mr Steer had intimated that his wife had been contemplating, if not actually having, an affair and that they had moved abroad in an attempt to patch up the marriage. I'm not sure what Mr Steer does business-wise, but in his notes from years back, it says that he was having panic attacks. Been playing dangerously with investments, I think, and had gotten himself in too deep. He mentioned it was a family business, so I assume that put a strain on everyone. Perhaps the break in India was to start a new business venture...'

'Or to escape some trouble here,' interjected James.

'Possibly. Well, Mrs Steer had been in and had confided in Linda that she was struggling. From the notes, although they're sketchy, it seems that Linda had discussed antidepressants, but Mrs Steer had refused them.'

James nodded. 'All sounds okay,' he said.

Cathy sighed. 'I wish Linda had documented the consultation in greater detail. I'll talk to her later about it, but I doubt she'll remember. It was over a year ago. At the end of her entry in the computer, it says that she handed Mrs Steer an information leaflet on domestic violence.'

'Oh, dear.' James shook his head. 'Alarm bells?'

'Exactly. I suppose I need to find out if she's in danger now. What if his story this morning was a cover-up of sorts?'

'You've called the out-of-hours folk?'

'I'm just off the phone.'

'Who was it that was on last night then? Perhaps they can help. If there was a call-out, at least we'd hear their side to it. Mr Steer might have been phoning making accusations and all sorts of nonsense, I suppose, and the information's just not come through from the evening's shift yet.'

Cathy was about to answer, but there was a knock on her door, and without waiting for an answer, it was opened.

'Oh, sorry to interrupt. I didn't realise. I had something to run by you, Cathy, but it can wait.'

Dr Euan Duncan smiled apologetically from Cathy to James. The newest practice partner was fresh-faced and only five years out of medical school. He had trained across in Dublin, where he had grown up, but on graduating, he had moved to Scotland for a change of scene. Everyone knew everyone back home, he had said, but he spoke of the place with a real fondness and regularly returned to visit.

Given his lack of experience, he had not been either Cathy or James's first choice initially when they had considered the applicants' CVs, but when he arrived for the interview, he had changed their opinion almost immediately. What he lacked in experience, Dr Duncan more than made up for in his enthusiasm. Cathy felt her spirits lift almost as soon as he had come into the meeting room that first day. When once both she and James would have sat doggedly attempting to wrangle through the intricacies of practice business, now, with Euan's slightly naive input, decisions seemed far simpler.

Cathy looked at her new partner now. He was about to close the door and his head of short, blond hair was bowed as he backed away. 'No, wait,' she called. 'Come in, Euan. Please. You're just the person I wanted to see actually.' Cathy raised an eyebrow at James, who in turn, raised his own, clearly understanding what she meant. 'I hear you were on-call last night, covering out-of-hours?' Cathy asked. 'I don't suppose anything exciting happened by any chance?'

4

Usually, she would have had the local radio station on to listen to the news as she returned home, but that evening after her late surgery, Cathy preferred to drive in silence. The night was cold and foolishly, she had not brought a jacket. Starting the engine, she immediately turned the heating up. The car moved forward, splashing in the puddles that had formed that afternoon. Her fingers ached with the thaw from the hot air now blasting from the vents in the dashboard.

On a normal day, the commute home to her small house on the outskirts of Glainkirk would take approximately five minutes. Today though, she had other plans but the visit she had been in part dreading would have to wait a little longer.

As she wound her way along onto the high street, turning onto Old Mill Road, she flicked on her windscreen wipers. They swished back and forth clearing her screen of a couple of leaves that had clung onto the damp glass. Before signalling at the end of the road, Cathy stared into the gloom. To the houses she passed, people would be returning home after work, with nuggets of stories to tell and gripes from the day to unburden on loved ones. Sighing heavily, she looked left and right, crossing the junction and again picking up speed. She was almost there. She counted the houses, unable in the half-light to see the numbers on the doors. She needn't have worried though. The front porch was illuminated and before the car had even pulled into the kerb, he was opening the front door to greet her.

Mr Earle beckoned her up the drive. She waved an acknowledgement and collected her bag from the back.

'Come in, come in,' he called, and Cathy, still at the bottom of the drive, heard the rasp of his breath. He cleared his throat and stepping back into the house, turned and called to his wife. 'She's here.' Coupled probably with the cold air, the exertion was too great for him. The elderly man began to cough. As Cathy hurriedly approached, he bent, his frail body racked with the effort of breath, his hands fluttering with the spasms.

'Let's get indoors,' she said calmly, and taking his elbow she guided him inside. Together they went through the hallway and she closed the door. 'It is rather chilly,' she said too cheerfully, as Mr Earle dabbed at his eyes with a large white handkerchief that he had produced from his trouser pocket. 'Not so good, then, yourself, Mr Earle? Are we heading through?'

Mr Earle raised his hand to indicate the way, although Cathy knew only too well having been many times before. 'Mrs Earle, how are you?' she said walking into the living room. They had the electric fire on and the old woman was stooping to press the switch.

'Don't!' her husband exclaimed, following the doctor in. 'I've told you already, you mustn't.' He came forward.

Mrs Earle tutted and sat down in the armchair once more. Her husband made his way across the room, stepping carefully as he crossed the worn hearth rug. Bending painfully, he finally stretched and flicked the switch that his wife had been reaching for. A third bar on the electric fire began to glow a warm orange gradually.

'Burnt herself the other day,' Mr Earle said in explanation, shaking his head. 'Doesn't think, do you, Nan? You don't think these days,' he said sadly, more to himself than his wife, or the doctor.

Mrs Earle shrugged her narrow shoulders but didn't answer.

'I'm afraid I've come at the worst possible time,' Cathy said, looking across at the folding table at the far end of the room. On it, were two plates. Cathy noted the half-eaten potted meat sandwiches and the smear of tomato ketchup on the side of one plate. Her heart lurched. A sad little meal. It was no wonder that Mrs Earle was losing weight. Cathy supposed that back in the day, it had been she who had cooked, but now, as her mind had begun to fog, her poor husband had taken on the burden. Mr Earle followed her gaze.

'Not at all,' he reassured her. 'Just a light supper. We don't eat so much in the evenings anyway, do we, Nan?'

Mrs Earle smiled vacantly and shook her head.

Mr and Mrs Earle were well-known to the practice. Both had grown gradually more infirm as the years passed and these days Cathy found herself doing house visits to them more frequently. Mr Earle gave her greater concern in many ways due to his worsening emphysema. The couple were in a precarious position. Mrs Earle had begun to show the early signs of dementia that year and her husband was her sole carer. Both were fiercely independent but Cathy wondered how long they could manage like this.

She spent a good half-hour with them, feeling guilty for not having been out sooner. They were, as always, pitifully grateful for her interest, even though she felt she did very little for them other than to sit and talk. Mr Earle was struggling, not just with his wife, but his own health. His face was red and mottled and his conversation as they sat before the fire, was punctuated by gasps. Cathy discussed organising more input from the social work department but he wasn't keen. 'We're managing fine for now,' he reiterated. 'I'll let you know if it changes, don't worry.'

But she did worry. It was tricky to know what to do for the best. Finally, Cathy suggested that she arrange a more thorough assessment to see if he might qualify for home oxygen and he at least agreed to that. Perhaps if she got him a little more comfortable, things might settle for a while. Inevitably, she knew that Mr Earle was going to die in the coming months, and unfortunately it would be well before his wife. Cathy looked at the woman, fragile and bird-like in her movements. She would end up being cared for in a nursing home with no relatives nearby. It was not what Mr Earle would have wanted for her.

Finally leaving them with the reassurance that she would visit again soon, she stood by her car and looked back at the house. Mr Earle had closed the front door but his wife watched unashamedly from the living room window. The elderly woman smiled and then seeming to hear something behind, turned. The folds of the curtain fell back and she disappeared.

Getting into her car, Cathy placed her doctors' bag beside her and checked her mobile. The out-of-hours doctors would be taking all emergency calls for her patients so the evening was in theory her own. Her stomach ached with emptiness. She'd not had a chance to grab lunch and had instead taken a couple of biscuits from the tin in the coffee room mid-afternoon. She could do with a coffee now. Her throat felt raw. When she got home, she'd run a hot bath perhaps and get an early night.

She turned the car slowly. Her final call before home was in quite the opposite direction. Travelling once again along the high street, she spotted a group of teenage lads jostling one another and raucously calling out. Cathy thought she recognised two of them. Rather than continuing onto Lanham Road, she signalled and turned up Mill Street and then left onto Ancrum Road. She'd not been out this way in some weeks but she knew the area well enough. This part of town was more affluent than where the Earles lived. The houses were well spaced and the drives were long. Since a heavy shower that afternoon, there had been no rain, though the moon was obscured behind clouds. The unvarying orange street lamps illuminated the puddled pavements but few people were out in this part of town.

As she drove, Cathy glanced from side to side. She quickly ascertained that the odd numbers were on the left, so focused her attention on that side. The house had a name, but she was looking for the number instead: 117. But it must be much further on: she was only at forty-nine.

Another car appeared in Cathy's rear-view mirror and she signalled, allowing them to pass. She was still unsure where she was heading and there was no reason to irritate fellow road users with her indecision. The car stayed behind her, despite her slowing and indicating to the left. Cathy tutted. 'Go past,' she grumbled. 'I'm letting you pass. What are you doing?' The car was now almost at a standstill behind her and she was forced to pull right in, giving the other driver no doubt as to her meaning. Finally, the car behind seemed to understand, and she shook her head as the dark saloon crawled past her own car, no doubt the driver looking in. 'I hope the police stop you. Your tail light's faulty,' Cathy said in annoyance. As she indicated to pull out again, she shivered.

It wasn't unusual to do late calls. She had done many in the past. Cathy covered some of the out-of-hours shifts too, but they were a little different as patients were either asked to come into the base, or the doctors had a designated driver with them if a visit was really necessary. Cathy preferred the camaraderie of having a driver. It was safer too, as in the car they carried resuscitation equipment and drugs. Many of the drivers did the job post-retirement to earn a little extra cash. Two had driven taxis in years gone by and all knew the area very well. Cathy, for the first time, wondered if Mr Steer's mysterious doctor had had a driver, if he had existed at all. As the afternoon had progressed, she had become more and more convinced that the man was indeed deluded and the entire story was fictional.

She had spoken with James. He had agreed that she couldn't leave it and should probably check, although had he known that she was going to be this late, he might well have advised her otherwise. The two doctors had listened to Euan's account of his previous night's work. Not once did he mention visiting anyone on Ancrum Road. Somewhat bemused by all the sudden interest, he told them that it had been a surprisingly quiet shift, despite the usual 'telephone dross,' he had called it. A young teenager with suspected mumps had come into the base. James had pricked his ears up at this. There had been a significant shortfall in the number of people accepting the MMR vaccinations. This had begun in 1998 following the press attention over a now completely discredited medical research paper linking the vaccine to autism. Since then, the general population had become warier of the vaccination programme. Numbers receiving the injections for measles, mumps and rubella had only recently begun to rise slowly. It was a relief given the seriousness of the diseases and the complications they caused. James had, for a time, been on a central committee trying to establish better uptake. Cathy knew that although James attended fewer medical council meetings these days, he was still very interested in the politics of the profession.

'You've reported the mumps case?' James had interrupted before Euan could continue.

The young doctor had laughed. 'Indeed, Dr Longmuir. It's the first one I've seen, so I got a bit excited, I'll admit.'

'Visits?' Cathy had asked.

'Only a couple. Can I ask, what's the cause of all the interest? I hope there's not been a problem.'

Cathy had smiled. 'Sorry. I didn't mean to sound like I was interrogating you. I don't suppose you were anywhere near the outskirts of town, on the road leading to the council tip?' Cathy knew that Euan was still finding his bearings since taking on the partnership. She had given him directions for a few visits already. Although most of their patients lived in the town itself, they did have a good number of people living more rurally. Cathy recalled that one of the visits Euan had asked for guidance on only a few weeks back had been off Ancrum Road heading east. It had been a farm and Cathy had ended up drawing a diagram to explain how to find it.

'The tip?' Euan asked, smiling in puzzlement.

'Well, I mean Ancrum Road. The long road you took to get to Mr Davies. Remember the old farmer with gout?'

'I know the man you mean. I did go out that way, as it happens. My driver was moaning about the late call. It was touch-and-go if it was us that went or the folks on the following shift. I thought it might be a quickie though and said I'd take it. Chest pain,' he said in explanation. 'It'd either be an ambulance or nothing. It turned out to be just a pleuritic, so no one was too late in finishing after all.' Euan paused, perhaps only thinking for the first time that there might be a real problem. 'Listen, has there been a complaint about me or something?'

Cathy shook her head. 'God, no. Don't panic. It's more than likely to be a mix-up. When did you clock off, Euan? You didn't do an overnight and then come in this morning, did you?'

'No. Goodness, no. I finished at eleven.'

Cathy sighed. 'That's a relief then. The time's wrong. He said it was nearly midnight when they came.'

Euan stood expectantly.

'I had a man in this morning,' Cathy finally explained. 'I've been discussing it with James just now. The man said that he had called the out-of-hours doctor to his house last night. It was a male GP, but the name the man gave didn't match up, and I wondered if he'd been muddled.'

Euan shrugged. 'Who was it? What was the call-out for?'

'It wasn't for him. It was his wife. She had a headache and a fever.'

'Had it been triaged as meningitis by any chance?' Euan asked.

'Why do you say that?' asked Cathy sharply.

'Oh, switchboard keep putting them through. I argued with someone the other night over it. Nearly everyone who calls with a rash, headache or fever seems to warrant an urgent call in case it's meningitis. I've dealt with far too many migraines and heat rashes since I've started working here. Things that could have waited until their own GP could see them in the morning.'

'Right. Funnily enough, the doctor who attended this man's wife, if he's to be believed, did think it was meningitis, but they had a rather odd way of dealing with it.' Cathy went on in response to Euan's raised eyebrows. 'Paracetamol and a cold bath. Yes, exactly,' she continued, 'but I have my doubts about the entire story. James and I were just wondering if the man who made the accusations might be unwell himself.'

'Paranoid delusions?'

'Perhaps. Who was it that took over from you last night, just out of interest, Euan?'

'Dr Kidd from the Westfield Practice. He's taking on a good few of the night shifts. Three young daughters to support. We were joking about it. But I think your first impression must be right. Dr Kidd would hardly advise putting a query meningitis in a cold bath. No medic would.'

'Nor would they lock the patient's husband in a spare room, only to disappear with his wife,' Cathy concluded to Euan's obvious astonishment. 'No. It needs looking into. I wish I'd not allowed the man to leave this morning now. The entire thing's ridiculous when you voice it out loud. I'm concerned for his wife too. The notes were sketchy, but apparently, Linda handed the wife an information leaflet on domestic violence the last time she was in. I'm starting to worry,' she had admitted to the two men.

Cathy now thought of her two practice partners who must both be home now, probably enjoying a glass of wine and their evening meal. How fortunate it had been to find Euan, but now with James's announcement, both she and Euan would be forced to begin the process again; advertising for another potential partner to join their team. Cathy didn't relish the task. She knew that they were unlikely to find as good a match for the practice. For the first time, as she drove, Cathy wondered if Linda, the practice salaried GP might apply for the post. She had been surprised that the woman hadn't considered trying out for the partnership before, but perhaps with a young family, she felt that the commitment was too great.

Cathy had, over the previous months, found herself distancing herself from Linda. Instead of sitting and enjoying the banter, she had begun taking her coffee downstairs to her room to drink in solitude, leaving the other doctor to cheerfully regale the rest of the coffee room with tales of her youngest son's faltering and amusing attempts to meet his milestones. Cathy herself was now in her mid-thirties and settling down with someone had evaded her thus far. There had been a couple of important people. The most recent, she had thought was going to be her last.

She had hoped... but it wasn't to be. He had enough issues of his own, without her adding to them. Her face felt scorched hot from the blast of the fan heater now. Hurriedly, she turned it off and refocused on the task at hand.

The street lights had come to an abrupt end and Ancrum Road snaked out into the countryside; two houses short of the number she had expected to find. Cathy drove on for a minute or so growing increasingly concerned. She was just able to make out the trees at the sides of the road and other large objects, barely seconds before her headlights gave them meaning and definition. She passed a small cottage and slowed down. Surely it had to be, but it wasn't.

Finally, she reached Balmuir House, a mansion that lay on the outskirts of Glainkirk town itself. She would have to turn around and go back. There was no way that this could be classed as the Ancrum Road any longer.

The surrounding land, Cathy knew, was well cultivated. She had taken walks around the area several times in the past. The house was privately owned, but at the time, as she had passed, she had peered up the drive and wondered about the upkeep and the family that lived there. So many windows to clean, and imagine the heating bills. Cathy didn't know the residents. She presumed they had registered with another practice, or perhaps they didn't bother with NHS doctors at all.

She knew that to the north of the mansion was a lodge house. A small solid stone building, built into the wall that surrounded the greater house. Cathy's headlights picked the cottage out on the left-hand side and slowing, she turned in, preparing to reverse and return the way she had come. From memory, the drive up to the big house was lined by tall trees. She could see little of them now though.

The road surface was no longer tarmac, and her car dipped suddenly into a pothole that had been filled to the top with rainwater. Cathy cursed, fearing her car's undercarriage might be scraped. Manoeuvring was easier given that the lodge house's porch light was on, and it gave her a better idea of the edges of the high metal gates on either side. It would be typical to reverse into one of them now to complete her bad luck. Before returning to the road, Cathy glanced into the cottage. One of the rooms was lit by a table lamp it seemed, but the curtains were drawn so that she couldn't see inside. It was only then that she spotted the sign to the right of the front door. It displayed no number, but astonishingly, the name of the house was the one she was searching for. She had found Mr Steer.

Her heart pounded in her temples, suddenly making her feel quite giddy. Turning off the car engine, she sat for a moment or two, trying to regain her composure. She had dealt with many difficult and mentally unwell people before. Why then was Mr Steer so different?

5

Mr Steer's house was well proportioned, perhaps more so than one might have expected for a simple lodge house. Cathy parked her car in the gap between the mansion's long drive and the hedge to the rear of the gates. She had already seen that there was no other car. As she had reversed, she had the sudden impression that something had moved at the window and she spun round to look through the passenger side. But there was nothing to see and the house looked the same as before. No one had come to the window to look, or opened the door hearing her approach. Feeling that her doctors' bag might make her feel more official, she reached over to get it.

The sky was now quite black with the moon completely concealed by a cloud. Guided only by the light from what appeared to be a front living room, Cathy crossed the drive, stumbling as she did so due to the uneven, gravelled path. She found her way to the front door which had no bell. Instead, she knocked and waited. She shifted her bag to her other hand. No sound came from within the house. Growing in confidence, she knocked again. He must have heard because she had rapped much louder than before. The sound rung out into the darkness.

Above her, the treetops rustled as they caught on the breeze and she heard the drip and tinkle of water as it ran into the gutters and drains of the house. No other car passed on the main road. Despite only being a minute out of town, Cathy felt quite alone.

After waiting a further minute, she tried the handle to the front door. She was now cold and her fingers slipped on the damp metal. The door did not open. She knocked again and then, with growing restlessness, she crept along the side of the house to the only window that was lit. Stretching along the side of the house was a flower border. Cathy hadn't realised until it was too late, and she stepped heavily into the sodden earth. Cursing, she continued along the wall of the house to the window. Of course, they grew roses. Twice she found herself pricked by thorns as they caught on her trouser legs. Drawing level with the room, Cathy leaned on the harled windowsill. The curtains, although drawn to, were not completely shut, allowing a sliver of light to escape. She peered in the window, her eyes blinked involuntarily, adjusting to the brightness. The glass slowly misted with her breath. She could see the brown and beige of a floral-patterned carpet, and as she moved further forward, craning in for a better view, she saw part of an armchair. The light caught the edge of a gilt picture frame on the wall at the far side. Cathy was now quite impatient. Her feet were beginning to feel the dampness of the ground and she was shivering uncontrollably. She tapped on the window.

'Mr Steer?' she called. 'Mr Steer, it's the doctor. Dr Moreland. Can you come to the door?'

It had begun to rain. She was sheltered by the house but a drip of water landed on her head and tracked down to her neck. She cursed. There was no way she could stumble about in the dark any longer. The whole thing was ridiculous. Cathy picked her way back to the car and got inside, dumping her doctors' bag on the passenger seat.

More than anything she wanted to start the engine and drive home. She was cold and hungry and a wave of self-pity suddenly reared over her. *Snap out of it,* she told herself. She had come because she had a duty of care to the man and the man's wife. She then remembered the torch in the boot. How stupid of her to forget. She again got out, screwing up her face in distaste as the rain whipped at her skin. She found the torch underneath a rolled-up blanket that she kept there for emergencies. She was just closing the boot and ready to return to the house when she heard a car coming. She saw the neon lights flickering intermittently between the trees as they approached. It was indicating left, just as she had done, and was slowing, the tyres swishing on the wet ground, and then crunching as they hit the gravel of the drive. Cathy stood frozen. The car's headlights caught her, blinding her completely. Then the driver was level with her and the window was wound down.

'Can I help?'

He was a man in his forties, she guessed. Quite dark, with a refined nose and a formed jawline that perhaps indicated a determined nature. She noted the expensive overcoat, the woollen scarf tied loosely around his neck. It certainly wasn't Mr Steer.

'I'm looking for Mr Steer,' she explained. 'I believe he lives here? The light's on, but he doesn't seem to be at home.'

The man glanced past her. 'No car. He must have gone out.'

'He does have a car then?'

But the car window was raised. The driver accelerated up the long driveway to the big mansion house, causing the car wheels to spin on the loose gravelled track.

Cathy stood miserably watching as the headlights continued up the drive. The beam caught on the tall trees as he made his way up to the house. Presumably it was his home. How rude of him, and how stupid she'd felt.

As if she needed any further influence, the rain began to come on more heavily. Mr Steer had left a light on and gone out. If Mrs Steer had returned to the house, she would surely have opened the door by now. As Cathy sat in the driver's seat once more and adjusted the heating, she reasoned with herself. Granted, she wasn't satisfied, but grubbing around in the dark, trying to peer into a patient's house, was hardly going to get her anywhere. Far better to return in the morning when it was light and to catch Mr Steer when he was certainly at home. *The leaflet*, a voice in her head said. *What about the leaflet Linda handed Mrs Steer? What if she is in danger and you've allowed it?*

Cathy groaned. She'd head up to the main house. Yes, the man who had driven past had been discourteous, but he might at least give her information and the peace of mind she needed.

Rather than making the awkward turn in the dark once more and doubting her driving capabilities to do so anyway, she walked the hundred metres. When she got there, she hovered uncertainly at the open front door. By the looks of things, the man who had just spoken to her was still unpacking his car. He had left the boot open and inside she saw a laptop case and cardboard boxes full of ring binders. Cathy climbed the stone steps and standing in the entrance, she saw that he had left the glass panelled door open also. Oh God, what would he think if he suddenly appeared and found her standing in his hallway? Cathy looked around for the bell, not wanting to appear furtive any longer than she had to, but as she located it, she heard a voice from within.

'Bloody hell!' a man said. His tone was full of anger, but Cathy thought he was trying to keep a lid on it. The voice went on, now hissing: 'But if anyone finds out, what are we going to do?'

Another man replied but the speech was more level. He

didn't attempt to lower his voice, but spoke calmly, as if to a child. 'You speak of choices...' he said.

Cathy froze, uncertain what to do. If she was about to interrupt a domestic, she felt uncomfortable. The voices seemed to echo. Were they standing right inside the hall with only the glass door between them? Cathy daren't look now for fear of being spotted. Instead, she shrank back against the cold stone pillar, her heart racing.

'Well, don't blame me,' the other voice countered. 'What else was I to do? The whole thing's as bad as it could be anyway. What choice did I have? Bloody cat. She deserved what she got.'

There was an ejaculation of exasperation but the man seemed to ignore this.

'Bloody cat,' he repeated sulkily. 'What the hell was she doing anyway? It was like she was on a mission to ruin both him and us. If she'd had her way, our entire business would be gone. Christ knows why she was in there. I can only assume it was at his bidding. Some sneaky deal. People never change. What about the precious third generation now?'

There was a pause and Cathy only heard the end of what was being said: '...else knows about it?'

Then the other man spoke and he sounded incensed. Their voices seemed even closer and Cathy held her breath, unsure what she should do. Now, certainly, would not be the time to be caught eavesdropping on the doorstep. She stepped slightly around the edge of the stone pillar by the left of the door, pressing herself into the building and the ivy that crept up it. As she had moved, a pebble scraped under her shoe. Cathy inwardly cursed. The voices inside stopped abruptly. She imagined the men looking towards the open door. Her heart was hammering so loudly in her ears that it was all she could do to stay upright. She looked skywards, holding her breath, and waited. The ivy leaves scratched at her neck, but she stood like a statue, trembling slightly against the cold wall. Dear God, what had she stumbled into? Who were these men and were they talking about Mrs Steer? She tried to focus. They were talking again.

'Just a bird, I think,' he said. 'Listen, I've been fielding calls all day trying to fight off overzealous... to find out the dirt... backstabbing bastards the lot of them! God alone knows what Dad would have said... loyal enough back then, but not when it comes to us. Even coming home... grubbing about outside their bloody house just now. A woman. Said she was looking for Mr Steer!'

Cathy held her breath and craned in, trying to hear the other man's answer. She heard a snort.

'No, I've no idea!' the other man answered. 'Never seen her before. Of course not. Stop being so bloody paranoid, how the hell would she? I told her to beat it, silly bitch. If I see her here again, I'll make sure she doesn't come back.'

Cathy grimaced in horror. What did he mean? Again, the other man spoke but she could only hear a mumble.

'No, well how the hell would anyone? No one knows. Only you and me and... Well, admittedly, he's the weakest link but there's nothing I can do about that unless you're suggesting... All right, all right... don't start getting like that. Money's a strong enough incentive for him undoubtedly, like all of these plebs. I'll see to it tomorrow and make doubly sure. I need a drink.'

Something else was said that she couldn't make out and then she saw a shadow moving on the stone steps. Realising that the man was now standing directly in front of the glass door, and blocking the light, Cathy knew that she had no choice but to move. She slid down the edge of the steps as quietly as she could and crouched down, hoping to go unseen. A large stone planter with a spiky bush was by the door and coupled with this and the ivy, she thought that he might not spot her. The door opened and the tall dark man she had seen earlier emerged. He stood at the top of the steps, hands on his hips. Cathy cowered in her hiding place, watching the mist of his breath as it touched the cold, night air. He tutted and then jogged down the steps to his car and, sighing heavily, removed his paperwork and bag, slamming the boot shut. Cathy shrank back, knowing that as he turned, he might see her. The ground was damp, but she barely noticed. The man glanced around once and then slowly retraced his steps.

Driving home, Cathy's stomach again lurched at the thought of what might have happened had she been discovered. And when she reached her driveway, she was horrified to see that it was far later than she had imagined. Locking the car, she glanced across at the neighbour's house. For once, the place was in darkness, and there was no sound. Since moving in, Cathy had been pained by the overenthusiastic people living next door. They were the kind that might proudly declare themselves as 'party folk,' despite being in their forties with two teenage children. The children weren't the problem though, it was very much the parents. Not wanting to be a killjoy, Cathy had ignored the late-night revelling, the revving of car engines as visitors came and went at all hours, the music blaring loud into the night. She had sat hunched in her own small three-bedroom house, wondering if she might ever get up the courage to confront them. She never had. Even when Chris had been there, she had often suggested that rather than make a fuss, they instead go to his flat. Cathy sighed. She rarely went out these days. Instead, she returned from work and slept. Her work had become her life. It always had been, but perhaps it was even more so now.

Cathy reached along the wall for the switch and the hall

sprung into light. Turning, she wearily closed the door behind, locking it and placing the chain on. She moved through the house, picking up the pile of mail by the door, having kicked off her soaking shoes. The floor felt cold even through her socks. She looked down and saw that these must have been thoroughly wet also, as she had left a track of damp footprints as far as the hall table where she now stood. Sighing, she dropped the mail and her keys. The clatter seemed to echo on forever. She'd get the heating on and the television. Although she despised the noise from the cheery neighbours, she could not abide silence in the house. She peeled her socks off where she stood and continued through, switching on lights as she went and going straight to the radiator in the living room to turn it to full. She stood there with her raw, red fingers wrapped around the top bar, waiting for the warmth to come like a pain. After a minute it did. The radiator ticked and she paused there, enjoying the throbbing heat on her hands. She pressed her back to the heater now also. She must get herself something to eat. A hot drink would help too. She felt again at her neck, her fingers now warm. The cervical lymph nodes were still raised and her throat felt dry. She was coming down with a virus, without a doubt.

Suddenly, more than anything, she wanted her bed. Her mind had been so active all day and returning home felt like suddenly a switch had been flicked. Her stomach rumbled and reluctantly she left the draw of the radiator and went through. A hot mug of tea would be comforting. Cathy filled the kettle and put a couple of slices of bread in the toaster. The kettle began to hum and the smell of the toasting bread lifted her spirits. Reaching into the cupboard for the box of teabags, her hand instead touched something else at the back. She knew what it was instantly and withdrew her hand as if burnt. Shaking her head, she reached up again and removing first the box of teabags, she then retrieved the bottle of vodka that had been behind them. She hadn't had a drink for over a month now. She had made a decision not to after Chris left, perhaps knowing how easily she might allow the habit to get out of control. She wondered if he had been as successful, but she doubted it. She held the half-empty bottle in her hands, allowing the clear fluid to slosh greasily up against the side. Smiling sadly, she replaced it at the back of the cupboard and shut the door. No, even though it had been a bad day, she'd not resort to that.

The kettle was beginning to reverberate and the toast was done. She buttered this, and hungrily took a bite. She tried to swallow, but the crumbs seemed to catch in her throat and clag. She abandoned the toast uneaten on the kitchen worktop, and instead, she took her mug of tea and a hot water bottle that she had had the foresight to fill also, and climbed the stairs. Tomorrow she would be able to think straight but now all she wanted was sleep.

6

The following morning, Cathy woke with the sun glancing through a chink in her curtains. The light fell in a distorted line across her bed and landed on her face making her squint. She stretched and shifted, turning lazily over and pushing the now lukewarm water bottle out and onto the floor. It fell with a hollow thump. She lay still and it was then that she remembered the reason for the underlying feeling of apprehension in her stomach. Today would be a better day though. Last night, she had simply been exhausted. This morning, she would return to Mr Steer's house. Now that she knew exactly where he lived, within no time, she would get to the bottom of the whole business. All she needed to do was to speak to the man. If she could just do that, it might all be resolved. With any luck, she'd avoid the people living up the drive at the mansion house. The conversation she had overheard troubled her. If they had been speaking about Mrs Steer, it did sound sinister.

'It will be fine,' she said aloud, and the sound of her voice in the empty house startled her.

She got up and showered. She stood for some time, allowing

the water to drum heavily on her scalp and shoulders. With her eyes closed, she turned her face to the water, enjoying the sensation as it scalded her cheeks and eyelids. The water roared in her ears and she considered the previous day's questions, and all that was still left unanswered. What would she find returning to Mr Steer that day? Would the man be angry for her interference? Would she expose him as a liar or a victim? She thought of Mrs Steer too, and although she hadn't met the woman, she felt a deep need to do so, to make sure that she was safe.

Reluctantly, Cathy turned off the shower and stepped onto the mat. She wrapped a large towel around herself and made her way back to the bedroom. She paused as she passed the dressing table, and impulsively opened the shallow drawer beneath. The wood caught and yelped in protest, but it came free and the inner was fully exposed. Beneath her jewellery box, Cathy fumbled for the edge of paper and finding it, slid it slowly out, taking care not to crumple the edges. She hadn't allowed herself to look at it in weeks. The envelope was crisp at the corners having been dampened and then dried out. It had been retrieved from her bin after she had tossed it there in a moment of furious self-pity. She was ashamed to have kept it. It showed that she hadn't moved on at all. Sitting at the low table now, Cathy pulled the towel tighter around herself and with pink, wrinkled fingertips, she opened the envelope, sliding out the note that he had left. Why was she torturing herself with this now? The paper creases clung together and as she pried them apart, her stomach flipped at the sight of his scrawled writing. There had been many. This was the one that she had kept though. It was short but the one that cut the deepest. Cathy's face was hot from the shower. She wiped her nose with the back of her hand as she read the words.

'Cathy. It was a mistake but a good one. We'll make it deliberately again, I promise.'

He had signed it with the letter 'C,' as he always did.

Sighing, Cathy replaced the letter in the envelope, sliding this under the jewellery box once again and closing the drawer. No good would come of this kind of nonsense and certainly not today of all days. She needed to have her wits about her.

Checking the time, Cathy dressed, choosing a pair of warm suit trousers. The band at the waist sagged and she reached for a belt. Giving herself a stern look in the mirror she decided that this morning she must force herself to eat, whether she was hungry or not. She pulled on a smart jumper and descended the stairs, picking a couple of bits of fluff from her as she went.

She lifted the kettle and filled it. From the kitchen window, she saw that the sky had cleared. The sun might finally find a proper break in the clouds and give the residents of Glainkirk some respite for the full day.

Leaving the house at exactly seven forty-five, Cathy pulled the jacket around her. Due to the break in the cloud, the morning was a frosty one, and the biting wind chapped at her hands and face. She pressed the key to her car. She'd have no time to go out to the Ancrum Road first thing and if Mr Steer was indeed at home this time, he might not thank her for the early call anyway. She had already decided that after her fully-booked morning surgery, she'd head out. Until then, she'd get through her work as best she could.

Cathy had begun her medical career some fifteen years ago. She was eighteen years old when she left home for medical school. Their first year had focused on the three major components to the subject: biochemistry, anatomy and physiology and she felt that she had truly found her place in the world. Back then, she had been so full of hot, idealistic desire to do good. She was the first in her family to go to university and the first in her school to study to become a doctor. The pressure of everyone's goodwill fell heavily on her, though, and rather than throwing herself into the raucous freshers' pub crawls, she had sat in her room in the halls of residence, poring over textbooks, trying to force the long words and complicated diagrams into her head. It was in her second week, and during an anatomy tutorial, that she had first met Suzalinna. The girl, who would go on to become a steady comrade throughout the five years of study and now far beyond, had smiled playfully at her. Despite arriving only six months before from India to begin the course, Suzalinna had the informal manner of someone who found her studies incredibly easy. Life was to be enjoyed and Suzalinna planned to make sure that she grabbed every opportunity. Soon the pair became inseparable and they made an unlikely duo; Suzalinna with her dark, mischievous eyes, and Cathy with her serious, pale, freckled countenance.

As Cathy pushed the door to the practice, she thought of her old friend Suzalinna. They had lost touch this past month. It was entirely of her doing and she felt dreadful for it. So many times, Cathy had sat with her finger hovering over the 'call' button, only to close her phone. Cathy missed her friend's affable chastisements, and her unfaltering confidence that at the end of the day, it would all be fine.

She saw James in the corridor twice during the morning as she greeted her patients, but both times he had a patient with him also and they were unable to speak, but he gave her the thumbs up and mouthed 'Okay?' Cathy nodded, but knew that she wouldn't be until she had spoken again with Mr Steer.

The morning seemed to drag. Cathy sat dutifully listening to her patients' troubles, but she knew she did them a disservice as her mind was elsewhere. Come half past ten, she took a look at the visits. James and Euan had already taken four of them, leaving her only one. Rather than join her partners for a coffee upstairs, she grabbed her car keys and bag, and left, slamming the heavy fire exit door behind her as she went. She would do the house call on the way. It sounded like a simple chest infection and might not take too long.

The roads were now greasy as the early morning sun had begun to thaw the frozen puddles that lined them. Cathy flicked on her windscreen wipers as the oily dirt from the roads was flung up whenever another car passed, smattering and obscuring her vision. She arrived at the house and having examined her patient and confirmed that she would indeed require an antibiotic, Cathy sat for a minute or two, in the living room. The woman had lit the fire the night before and in the grate, the dusty, grey embers still waited to be raked. Cathy shivered and looking up, realised that she'd missed the question she was being asked.

'I'm sorry, Mrs Grant,' she said, knowing that the woman was unlikely to have another visitor that day. 'What was it you were saying?'

The old lady shook her head. 'Working yourself half to death,' she repeated. 'I've seen it before. Let me make you a sandwich before you go.'

Cathy smiled and stretched out a hand. 'I'm fine.' But the woman wasn't a fool. She grasped Cathy's hand between her knuckled fingers and squeezed it with surprising strength.

Having arranged for a prescription of amoxicillin to be left at the reception desk for the lady's chemist to collect later, Cathy gathered her stethoscope.

'Take care of yourself,' Mrs Grant called after her as she walked away down the drive.

Cathy smiled thinly at the irony of the statement and at that moment, wanted nothing more than to get in the car and drive home, back to her empty cottage. But it had to be faced, and why she dreaded the damn thing, she couldn't say. It was part of the job, taking responsibility for one's actions and keeping people safe. That was all she was doing. Returning to Mr Steer's house to sort the confusion out.

She didn't allow herself to think it through any longer and instead made her way back out onto Ancrum Road with the radio blaring to drown out the voice in her head that told her not to go. Despite her misgivings, she forced herself to admire the scenery as she drove. How different it all looked in the daylight. As she reached the end of the houses and continued out into the countryside she wondered at how much closer to town the mansion house seemed. With the lodge house upon her before she knew it, she hurriedly indicated.

Almost immediately, she saw that there was no car again. Her heart leapt in elation. Maybe he wasn't home. But, of course, that was stupid. She needed to speak to him. That was the whole reason for coming. Mr Steer might still be at home, she reasoned, although she had already spotted that this time, there was no light on.

Cathy parked and went to the front door. The sooner it was over with, the better. Once again, she waited. Frustrated, she shifted from foot to foot and saw to the right of the door the flower border and in it a deep footprint, evidence of her mishap the night before. Beside it, she was intrigued to see, was another print. It was from a much larger foot, and presumably a man's. *How odd*, she thought. The only reason to have stood there would be to look in the window as she had done. She knocked again but she knew in her heart that there would be no answer. Perhaps this gave her greater confidence. Perhaps she knew she'd not have to meet Mr Steer again that day. With far more poise, as she was able to see her path this time, she made her way slowly around the house. She pulled the folds of her jacket around her waist, treading cautiously as she moved, first coming to the window she had peered into the previous evening.

44

Cathy's eyes grew wide and she blinked stupidly for some moments in incomprehension. The blood drained from her face and involuntarily, she grabbed at the wall, swaying. Her knuckles grazed the stony pebble-dash of the building and she looked down at the ooze of red that had already sprung from her hand.

'It can't be,' she said to herself.

She looked around her as if trying to find an explanation but no one was there and the road was empty. She was in the right place. This was the correct house. To the left was the drive leading up to the great mansion house, just as it had been last night. Why then was the room she looked into entirely bare? The curtains that had been hung the previous night had been removed. The armchair that she had seen through the gap in the material and the picture with the glinting frame had gone also. Even more shockingly, the carpet, the beige and brown flowery carpet that she could still picture in her head had been lifted. The room was an empty shell. The walls were void of hangings, and the floorboards lay unadorned.

'I must be going mad.' Her breath had quickened and it came in a clouded mist before her. 'My God, but how?'

Her feet seemed rooted to the spot and she had no idea how long she stood, but before long, the cold crept into her, making her joints throb and her lungs ache. She moved her weight gradually, afraid that she might cry out in pain, or collapse. It had been the wrong window, she told herself. Although glancing down, she again saw her own footprint from the night before and knew she was not mistaken.

And then, with sudden urgency, Cathy began to pace around the outside of the house, keeping clear of the borders this time, and stepping out onto the lawn. The leaves that had fallen from the surrounding trees crunched underfoot as the sun had not spread this far. Once she leapt in fright, thinking she had trodden on something that moved but shaking her head, she continued, stepping out onto the gravel and around the house. She looked into each window in turn, pausing, surveying and moving on, hoping with all her heart to find something to explain the circumstances. But with growing dread, she made a full circuit of the lodge.

Every room was bare. Not a piece of furniture, not a scrap of evidence that anyone had ever lived there.

7

S he didn't remember getting back into her car, but shivering now quite uncontrollably, she rested her hands on the steering wheel and tried to think. How long she sat like that she didn't know, but her head suddenly jerked at the sound of a car engine starting. She looked in her rear-view mirror, assuming that the vehicle must surely come from the big house, but to her astonishment, a set of headlights appeared through the gaps in the trees and the car slowly approached along the main road, driving out of Glainkirk. Cathy couldn't understand. She had certainly heard the engine being started. What had the driver been doing parked there at the side of the road? She hadn't heard or noticed the car before. How long had they watched?

As the car neared the turning to the mansion house, it slowed even further, until it was at a crawl going by the gates. Cathy wondered if they would turn and come up the drive. Had they been lost, or too early for an appointment? Confused, Cathy peered through the misted windscreen, but she was unable to see if it was a man or a woman. As if realising that they had been seen, the driver suddenly accelerated, not driving up the long sweeping driveway at all, but continuing along the main road and out of town. The car's wheels spun, scattering loose stones like hail. Cathy sat motionless, watching as it disappeared over the brow of the hill. She'd spotted the faulty tail light almost at once. It was just as she had seen the previous night. It could hardly be a coincidence. Undoubtedly, either she or the mansion house was being watched.

Starting the car engine, she sighed. She must get back to work. All the way, she turned the impossible matter over in her mind. The car was, in truth, a minor matter in comparison to the rest. How could it have been empty when only twelve hours before she had looked in those windows and had seen the place furnished? Again, and again she recalled the lamp, the armchair, the picture and the carpet. Why would anyone move out so rapidly, ripping up all evidence of their existence, even the carpets? It seemed utterly absurd. The entire business was absurd. The man's story about his wife's disappearance, the strange doctor who was meant to have called himself 'Dr Hope', and now this.

By the time she arrived back at the practice, Cathy had begun to wonder if she had met Mr Steer at all, or if the tale had been some kind of nightmare or mind trick of her own making. She was no longer frightened but strong indignation had taken hold. What was going on, and why was she involved in it? All she was trying to do was keep her patients safe, and she had ended up in the middle of some impossible puzzle. The whole thing was infuriating. In reality, she should have been thinking about advertising for a new partner to replace James. She should be spending her evenings drawing up a list of requirements for the future doctor and discussing the business with Euan to gauge his thoughts. Her life was busy enough with work, without adding to it.

She leaned her shoulder against the heavy door at the back of the building and made her way through the corridor that led to her room. She would have welcomed the cheerful nod from a colleague, but on either side, the doors were closed. She arrived at her own and unlocked it, flicking on the light. She flopped into the seat by her desk and sighed heavily. The radiator behind her clunked and she instinctively swung around in alarm at the sudden sound but shook her head in disgust. *Ridiculous*, she thought to herself. She was no use to her patients like this.

Getting up, she paced the room. She stood absent-mindedly on the scales but didn't need to look at the reading. She already knew simply from her reflection in the mirror that morning, that she had lost more weight. Even her patients were noticing. She pictured Mrs Grant. 'Working yourself half to death,' the old lady had said. Perhaps she was right.

She could hear her friend Suzalinna's voice in her head too. She would have been furious with how bad things had become. Cathy could hear her friend's lilting Indian accent scolding her: 'You need to look after *you*,' she would have said. 'You're no use to anyone unless you're fit and well yourself.' But it was always the way when she was overwrought or anxious, her appetite was the first thing to go. Since finishing with Chris, she had dropped at least half a stone, if not more. In that time, she had found herself distancing herself from her friends also and had instead, retreated into the regularity of her work. She had offered to take on more than she should in the practice simply to keep herself busy and to numb herself to the inevitability of returning to an empty house. And then she thought of the empty house she had just visited and her stomach lurched with the reality of what she had seen.

Cathy sat down heavily once more. Either she was indeed going completely insane, and admittedly she had come pretty close a couple of years back, or there was a more rational explanation for the strange events. Cathy logged on to her computer to see how busy the afternoon looked. She noted that her first patient had arrived early and was already waiting. Although torn, she decided that they could sit a little longer. She turned her thoughts again to the bizarre events of the past few days. It seemed that, bar her insanity, the only conceivable possibility was that Mr Steer had fabricated the entire story about the doctor and, with a history of violent behaviour towards his wife, he had used the ridiculous tale as some kind of excuse or cover-up for her disappearance. Possibly, he had killed her.

Cathy again felt her stomach heave. Dear God. If he had, she might never forgive herself for allowing him to leave her consultation room, free to potentially kill again. If it turned out he was a murderer, might he then have perhaps thought better of sticking around himself? Had he scarpered, taking everything that had belonged to them with him? Maybe him reporting the odd circumstances to the police and her was part of the plan, to absolve him of any suspicion and to make it seem as if he too had been kidnapped. And that of course, was the second option and just as dreadful in reality. Was it even imaginable that it wasn't only Mrs Steer who had been abducted, but now her husband also?

Cathy snorted. Even the fact that she was considering these things was ridiculous. Murderers, kidnappers? Who on earth would want to kidnap the Steers and for what possible reason? It was the sort of thing that might happen in some gangster film, where organised crime was endemic and mob warfare the norm.

'This is Glainkirk,' Cathy said aloud.

Had the house not been empty, she might well have been able to leave the thing. She might have concocted a story for herself to make it fit. She'd say to James that she was going to assume that Mr Steer had made a bit of a mountain out of a molehill. She could quite well imagine Mr Steer feeling embarrassed about coming in to see her. Both she and the police had been a mistake on his part. His wife had run off with some man and this whole nonsense over the out-of-hours doctor had been a simple misunderstanding. He'd made an utter fool of himself. He hadn't been locked in his spare bedroom at all. The door had simply jammed shut and while the doctor had finished assessing his wife, who, as it turned out, wasn't so unwell as she had made out, she had left. She hadn't bothered to explain the thing to him. He'd been bulldozing her all this time, forcing her halfway across the world in an attempt to get her away from temptation, but arriving home, it had been too much, and she had snapped. These kinds of things happened all the time. Families were odd, and no one knew what was going on within a marriage. Often, even one of the spouses didn't realise until a crisis was upon them. Cathy thought sadly of her own relationship. She too hadn't known until it was too late. She shook her head, trying to erase the image of Chris as she bent to get into her car, outside his house. Their eyes had met and she had turned angrily and slammed the car door, setting her teeth on edge and making herself flinch.

But this wasn't about her.

What was it that Mr Steer had said again? Something about working long hours and not giving his wife enough attention. Perhaps it was far worse. Mrs Steer had lived a lonely existence, having been isolated by her husband's controlling nature. She had been forced into the shape of someone she didn't want to be. When her ego-fuelled husband had come home from his important business meetings, he had been dismissive. He had patronised her and made her feel worthless and unloved. That was what had driven her to look elsewhere. And that was why she'd left without explanation. She knew he'd never let her go without a fight.

Mr Steer had known all of this when he came to the GP

surgery that morning. He had been deluding himself, too narcissistic to admit that his wife had gone of her own choosing. Of course, no woman would want to leave him. The only explanation was that she had been taken. Perhaps only then, returning home to his empty house, so full of the memories of his wife, he had cracked and had a bit of a breakdown.

Cathy liked this story. It made sense to her and it absolved her of any guilt. She'd not been wrong to send Mr Steer away and she'd not endangered him or the general public in doing so. She could continue her work that day without concern or blame.

But what about the empty house, and what about the man's footprint in the flower border by the window? Well, even that could be explained, Cathy remonstrated. He'd cleared out, of course. The footprint had been there for months and was unrelated. The memories of his failed marriage were too painful and he had probably decided that India hadn't been so bad after all. He'd only just come back himself. He'd been over there for some time and had made strong alliances. Those friends and perhaps work associates would buoy him through his marriage failure. In India, the culture was quite different. He would be respected and revered. Perhaps on his return, and after a respectable length of time following his divorce, he'd find a good woman. Someone who would have his meals on the table when he came home, someone who would listen to his worries and compliment him on his intelligence in business. Yes, this all seemed good.

What about the carpet, a sly whisper asked?

Damn the blasted carpet, she wanted to reply angrily. *Damn it, and the horrible, bloody curtains too.* But she knew it wouldn't do. However tight and appealing the story was, it couldn't allay the nagging doubt. It was true that Mr Steer might have cleared out and gone, but to lift the carpets and tear down the curtains did seem a bit much. And what of the odd conversation up at the mansion house that she had overheard? Was it even related to the Steers? Cathy sat for a few minutes wrestling with the problem, but knowing full-well what the outcome must be. She couldn't let it drop, no matter how much she wanted. She was way beyond that now.

8

Cathy glanced again at the computer screen. She guiltily ignored the highlight on the monitor indicating that now her second patient sat awaiting her attention just along the corridor. Sliding her chair back, she crossed the corridor and tapped gently at the door diagonally opposite hers. There was a pause and then, hearing the answering greeting, she went in. It was ludicrous really, but her heart beat faster. *No going back*, the voice in her head said. Once she started digging, that was it.

Linda had been a member of the practice for over three years now. She had originally joined as a GP retainer, a position held by doctors returning after a break from medical practice, often due to pregnancy. She had taken a full year away initially following the birth of her first child and had only returned to announce another pregnancy within a couple of months. Cathy, who had been her assigned mentor, had been a little disappointed. She had put a good deal of time and care in devising a training regimen for the woman, and to then find out that it might all be wasted if she forgot it once again on maternity leave, made her somewhat dispirited.

Linda had, in the end, taken six months leave the second

time around and had come back even more rusty, which wasn't as great a problem as her new-found fear of making a mistake. This fear took the form of endlessly over-investigating her patients and Cathy lost count of the times she had been forced to step in, seeing an inappropriate referral dictated for one of Linda's patients to be assessed up at the hospital. As well as running her own busy surgeries, Cathy had come to accept that her door might be knocked upon umpteen times a day with a request from Linda for a 'quick question' or a 'wee second opinion'. Cathy had been infinitely patient with the woman, but it had started to wear thin.

In fact, the strain of dealing with Linda's insecurities had taken its toll on Cathy. Too many times she had been forced to make decisions for her more cautious colleague. Having said that, when Cathy had herself to go off sick due to mental health issues, Linda had surprised everyone. She had stepped up with astonishing eagerness and had covered the shortfall of sessions until Cathy was fit to return. They had all been grateful. Locums were hard enough to come by, so to have someone reliable and known to the patients already, was a blessing, even if she did need some extra reassurance from her colleagues.

Despite this, Cathy still had her doubts as to whether Linda would be a suitable partnership candidate when James retired. She had been thinking about it these past few weeks, turning the thing over. She worried about how she and Euan should react to Linda's interest in the post if she did express it. She was adequate as a salaried employee. She was punctual and only rarely called in to say that she couldn't come to work due to one of the kids being sick. She did have to finish bang on six, though, and there was no negotiation with this. It was because she had to collect her children from the local nursery. Her husband worked away often and couldn't do it himself. But being a salaried member of the practice was somewhat different to becoming a partner. The responsibilities of the partnership were something else. Perhaps it was unfair, but Cathy couldn't shake the image of Linda standing at her door only a year or so ago, almost in tears due to her inability to decide what to do with a patient. It was a part of the job that you either accepted or fought against. There would always be uncertainty in everything they did as doctors. Cathy acknowledged that this was why their profession earned a good deal more money than many others; because of the weighty responsibility that rested on them. Other people could go home and forget about their day's work of an evening, but Cathy knew that very few of her colleagues would ever truly switch off. She rarely did.

'Sorry, Linda,' she said, 'I know we're all about to start our afternoon surgeries, but I wondered if you had a sec?'

Linda, who had been by the sink, shook the water from her hands and reached for a paper towel from the dispenser on the wall. 'What's up, Cathy?' she asked. 'Problems? I've not put my foot in it again?'

Cathy grimaced. It was so typical of Linda to be on the defensive right from the word go. 'No, you've done nothing wrong,' she said. Her voice wavered slightly and the other woman shot her a glance. Linda crossed the room, her wrap-around dress clinging to her ample form.

Deciding to skip the whole bizarre story, Cathy took a deep breath. 'There's nothing wrong,' she lied. 'I was just wanting some background on a patient. I was wondering if you had any recollection of a woman you saw a few months back. I know it's a long shot, but do you recall a Mrs Steer? Marjorie?'

The other doctor paused and then depressed the pedal on the bin with the toe of her boot. It clanged against the wall loudly. 'Yes,' she said simply. 'I'm awful with names, but I do know Marjorie. Why? Is she back from her travels yet? It was meant to be India, wasn't it?'

Cathy inhaled. She hadn't expected Linda to recall the consultation at all.

Linda had now seated herself. She shuffled the chair forward and adjusted the hem to her skirt which had ridden up to her thigh. Cathy watched her colleague's movements; all she knew to be subconscious tells to reassure. They were both anxious, Cathy decided. But both for a different reason. Linda tilted her head to one side. Her full lips were just parted.

'She has come back, apparently,' Cathy said. 'Well, that's if her husband's to be believed, I suppose, which at the moment, I'm unsure about, and I can't even find him now, for that matter...' She tailed off and rolled her eyes, annoyed. 'If you can tell me about the family it might help.'

Linda exhaled slowly. 'I'll tell you everything I know about Marjorie. I've never met him, though. I know her through the gym,' she explained. 'I saw her professionally in here a while back. She was mildly depressed. Didn't want antidepressants, if I remember right. I think she said there were some serious problems at home but she didn't go into it too greatly with me. I saw her at the gym a few weeks after that. I was there with Lucy. They run a baby yoga class and I was taking her to it and bumped into Marjorie in the foyer.'

'And she mentioned her trip abroad then? Was it only the once you saw her at the gym?'

'Maybe a couple of times. I've seen a few patients there. She mentioned that they intended on going but if I'm honest, I wasn't too convinced. I got the impression that she was all talk, if you know what I mean? Someone you don't take too seriously. When she said India, I thought it was a bit out there, you know? She said that the husband had had some offer of work and that she was going to be doing something too. She was excited. Said it was a fresh start for them. I wasn't all that attentive. Yoga was just starting up and the place was mobbed with mums and kids.'

'Do you know what her profession was? I think her husband's something business-related.'

'Oh, he is. I think he had a bit of a fall from grace though and that was a big part of the reason for the move. He used to be the CEO for Traxium, same company as Pete, funnily enough.'

'What? The pharmaceutical empire? I didn't even realise your husband worked for them.'

'He's been a drug rep for them for several years now. The job's been fine for him anyway. Good pay and he likes the travel, but it doesn't fit in with the childcare issues, as you can imagine.'

Cathy nodded. 'So, Mr Steer was your husband's boss?'

Linda shook her head. 'No, not directly. I don't think they would have ever met, to be honest. It's such a big company. Pete mainly deals with flu vaccines in the UK. Traxium has been vying for the top distribution deal for years but they keep falling short. They have laboratories and investments all over the world though. I'd guess that the Steers must have been rolling in it at one time. That was partly why Marjorie was so depressed, well that's what I thought, reading between the lines. She'd given up work and was at home, rattling about that mansion place with nothing to do. She'd been a photographer, I believe. We spoke about her taking it up again, even as a hobby when she was depressed.'

'So, she and her husband lived in the mansion at one time?'

'I believe so. I don't think the wealth suited her though. Some people who aren't born into it, I suppose...'

'You said that you weren't convinced she'd go abroad at all. Why then, did you ask me at the beginning if she was back?' Cathy bit her lip. This sounded like an interrogation and she hated herself for being so tactless, but Linda hadn't seemed to notice.

'Oh, gym gossip, I'm afraid.' Linda laughed, and her plump cheeks grew a deeper red. 'I got the rest of the story from another mum. She saw me talking to Marjorie and thought I knew all about it what with being a doctor too. Marjorie was having an affair,' Linda explained. 'I heard that they'd gone. Presumably, her husband thought it was the only way to keep his wife from running off with her fancy man. Very unhealthy relationship.'

Cathy swallowed, disliking the ease with which Linda had descended into hearsay about her patient, but if she had more to divulge, Cathy would not find out. Both of the women started at the sudden ring from the telephone on Linda's desk.

Linda rolled her eyes and snatched it up. She groaned. 'All right,' she said and replaced the receiver. 'Baying for blood, according to reception. Better crack on.'

Cathy nodded and moved to the door. She felt a little nauseous. As she crossed the corridor to her room once more, she saw Euan as he too headed into his room. Euan must have caught a glimpse of her also, because he leaned back in the doorway and smiled at her, his face boyish and charming. He clung to the edge of the door and then apologising to someone within the room, came back up the corridor towards her.

'Cathy,' he said. 'Cathy? Are you all right? I just thought you looked a funny colour.'

Cathy smiled and brushed her hair off her face. 'Thanks. I'm okay.'

He nodded. 'Pale, very,' he said and pointed to her face. 'Maybe bloods?'

Cathy shook her head. 'Honestly, I'm fine.'

As she returned to her room, she wondered if Euan's on-call driver had noticed anything suspicious as they drove past the mansion house on the way to or from the late visit that night. Even a car parked outside the Steer's house might take Cathy further. It wouldn't be so hard to find out which driver had been on with Euan. She could of course easily approach Euan after their afternoon surgeries had finished, but she didn't want her partners to think she was obsessing over the case. Cathy had a scientific mind. She thought with strong logic and intelligence but that didn't prevent her from trusting gut feeling. In many ways, it was this sensitivity that made her an excellent doctor in the first place. Since she had been diagnosed with bipolar disorder, she had noticed a heightening of these senses. No, she'd trust in her intuition and not approach Euan that day.

As she greeted her first patient, Cathy knew what she must do next. She had two lines of inquiry to explore now. She must find out more background on both of the Steers, and she was particularly interested in the man with whom Mrs Steer was meant to have been having an affair. Then there was the night in question when Mr Steer claimed that he had called the out-of-hours GPs. That needed further attention.

'Mrs Sturrage, come in, come in. So sorry to keep you. Been rushed off our feet today,' she apologised, and her voice told of a new confidence and determination.

9

'Well,' Dave said, removing his glasses and rubbing them on the hem of his jumper. 'I'd need to think, right enough. Last week? I'm all over the shop, I can't tell you what I did yesterday. Truth is that Sheila was taken to hospital only the week before. Legs again.'

Cathy nodded. 'Sorry, I didn't realise.'

'No, no,' he said, waving her sympathy away as if batting at a fly. 'Just the way things are at the moment, but I could have done without the shifts this week. Same as you doctors though. Can't get anyone to do a swap, especially not at short notice. Not that I'm complaining. We need the cash, me and Sheila, so I've been visiting the hospital late afternoon and having to leave her without any company on the nights I'm here.'

Cathy smiled. She'd known Dave Ramage and his family for the full seven years she'd been a partner, having opted in to be part of the out-of-hours team. It wasn't a necessity for the GPs to cover the shifts, but Cathy had felt it important to keep her hand in. She rather enjoyed the variety of the work and when she had first moved to the area, she had learned a good deal from her drivers about the quickest routes in and around the town. She had met Dave's wife, Sheila, professionally a few times when she had been working on the out-of-hours service. Both Dave and his wife were registered with the Westfield Practice as they lived some way out of town. But whenever Cathy was on a shift with Dave, she would always ask after her. Being a diabetic, she'd been having problems with leg ulcers for a couple of years now. She was only in her late fifties and Cathy hadn't realised things were so hard for them recently.

'You must say I was asking for her,' she told him. 'Maybe I'll pop in on the way home one evening. Do you know how long she'll be in the hospital?'

'Couple more days, I think. Badly infected this time. Didn't bother the Westfield lot with it. We knew ourselves she'd need to stay in and I took her straight to the ward. They didn't mind,' he added.

'Good,' she said and then keen to get back to the reason for her questioning, she paused. Her face felt suddenly hot. He must have realised that she was struggling because he looked at her, tilting his head to the side.

'What day was it again?' he asked, saving her the embarrassment of repeating her question.

'This last week. It was the Tuesday. Dr Duncan was on that night,' she said, hoping to jog his memory. 'I believe it was Dr Kidd from the Westfield Practice who took over after that. That's what Euan said, but I've not seen the rota to confirm.'

'Dr Kidd's been picking up a fair few recently. I'm not surprised it was him on after. Must be short on cash like me.' He laughed. 'A few of the drivers have been a bit worried about him actually. Taking on too much and then going into work straight from an all-nighter here. Some of the nights have been busy too and he should be heading home to his bed, not going into a full day's graft. Not good for him or his patients, that's what they've been saying, some of them.'

'Oh dear,' Cathy said. 'That doesn't sound so good. I've not seen Dr Kidd in a few months. I can look into it if you think...?'

But the man was shaking his head. 'Not me,' he said. 'I'm not part of it. It's Christopher and Maurice who were talking about it, not me at all. I don't stick my nose in. I've got enough to worry about myself.'

'Getting back to the night in question,' Cathy said, now no longer abashed at moving the conversation along. 'It would have been a night you'd remember because Euan said that there was a bit of to-ing and fro-ing about who should take the late call. By rights, it had come in on Euan's shift, but driving out there would have taken a bit of time and, in theory, Dr Kidd could have done it as soon as he came into the base.'

'I'm not sure...'

Cathy knew that she sounded desperate. 'It was a chest pain,' she interrupted. 'Out on the Ancrum Road and beyond so Euan said. I'm not sure how far. I should have asked.'

Dave chuckled. 'I'm losing my marbles. Now you say it, of course, I remember. We'd had a nice little shift that night and Dr Duncan had been kind enough to pop out and buy the pair of us a fish supper. A thoughtful gesture, that was. He'd no need to do it, and he'd not take a penny from me. The Haven,' he said in explanation. 'They do good chips if you're ever needing.' He looked her up and down, perhaps judging by her frail frame that she could do with the odd greasy meal.

But Cathy was growing impatient now. She had come to the out-of-hours base hoping to find answers, not gain recommendations of where to buy her takeaways.

'It was simply about that late call,' she persevered. 'I wondered if while you were out driving, you'd seen anything odd on the way up Ancrum Road. Do you know the big old mansion house? I forget what it's called. Bal-something?'

'You'll mean Balmuir House, I suppose?'

'Yes,' Cathy spoke excitedly. 'Yes exactly. It would be somewhere around about there. I was thinking you might have spotted a car parked at the gates to the lodge or any movement around there. Presumably, the road's usually very quiet at that time so any traffic would be unexpected.'

'It would,' Dave admitted. 'And I do remember the night in question, but I can't help you at all.'

Cathy was crestfallen. But it had been foolish of her to think otherwise, and what had she thought poor Dave was going to say? That he'd seen someone impersonating a doctor, carrying Mrs Steer, bound and gagged to their car? 'Nothing unusual then?' she asked pathetically.

'Well, I couldn't say, could I? It wasn't me.'

Cathy, whose gaze had been cast down at her feet, looked up again sharply. 'What do you mean, it wasn't you? Did the nightshift driver take Euan instead to the last visit so you could get away home?'

Dave shook his head. 'I know it's against policy, but when he said it, it made sense. He'd be heading back, you see? Right in that direction to his own home and was as well travelling it himself. Said he'd record it all in the morning.' Dave looked sheepish. 'I hope I've not gotten him into trouble. It seemed the right thing for everyone, you see? Dr Kidd could start his shift without rushing out.'

Cathy needed to be sure she'd understood. 'Are you saying that you didn't drive at all? And that Euan, alone, in his own car, drove to the final visit off Ancrum Road that night?'

'As I said, I know doctors shouldn't go to calls alone due to the risk, what with the drugs and all that, but it made perfect sense for him to do it. I think he dropped off the drug bag on the way into work the following morning. That's what he said he'd do. Dr Kidd knew about it and didn't seem fussed. Probably glad not to have to go out and do the call himself. Chest pain right as soon as you start a shift can't be much fun. I think he must have been hoping for a quiet one that night.'

'Thanks,' Cathy said absently.

Her mind was frantic with questions, none of which Dave could answer. She simply couldn't understand. Euan had had every opportunity to tell her the truth when she questioned him about the visit but he had chosen not to. Had it been because he was breaking out-of-hours protocol and doing a late visit alone, carry the emergency drug bag with him when it should never really leave the driver's side? Cathy hoped that it was simply this because the alternative was something quite different and infinitely more troubling. For the first time, Cathy was forced to consider if Euan Duncan, her own practice partner, might have been passing the Steer's house that fateful night after all.

10

'Returned home? What? Home, as in back to Dublin?' Cathy asked in disbelief.

'Last minute flight. He left a message.' Michelle, the lead receptionist seemed to enjoy the effect her words had and pursed her lips in satisfaction. 'His grandmother. She's gravely unwell. I've managed to rearrange most of his mornings already. Everyone's been incredibly understanding when I've told them the reason.'

'I'm sure they have,' Cathy said, knowing only too well that she sounded annoyed. She was aware that even after a very short spell working at the practice, Euan had collected himself a strong and faithful following. Many seemed to be elderly women who naturally fell for his charming patter. Both she and James had laughed about it in the past, highlighting to Euan that, come Christmastime, despite being the newest partner, he would undoubtedly receive the most cards and home-baked treats from the patients. 'I suppose we'll have to cope,' Cathy said. 'I'd been needing to speak to him about something important. It's bad timing and all very unfortunate.'

The receptionist shrugged. No doubt she was eager to continue with her rearrangements, distributing those patients that had been urgent, to Cathy, Linda or James. The others who wanted to see Euan, in particular, might hold out until he returned. It was all rather inconvenient.

Cathy found herself in James's room after they had finished their morning surgeries. It did little good discussing it but Euan's sudden absence bothered her. 'It's a bit of an unexpected way of doing things though,' Cathy said, still irked by the news, having stewed over it all that morning. 'I mean, why didn't he call you or me? We're his partners and to simply leave a message on the practice answering machine for one of the girls to pick up seems a little... I hate to say it but, well, a little unprofessional.'

James cleared his throat and Cathy wondered if he minded quite as much. 'At any rate,' he said. 'We've covered the shortfall today. The girls at reception have phoned around. There was only a couple they didn't manage to get hold of. If they turn up for their appointments with Euan, I'll see them myself, don't worry.'

'Oh, it wasn't that, James,' she said, hoping he didn't think her that petty. 'You know I don't mind seeing folk and mucking in; it's just the whole way of going about things. It just doesn't sit too well.'

'He's young and new to the partnership,' James said, meditatively. 'He'll realise when he gets back that he made a bit of a blunder. He was probably in a panic trying to arrange flights and left calling us until he'd got that sorted. No doubt he'll be back in a day or so. It's extenuating circumstances. You or I might have a quiet word with him when he returns, but I suppose, if a close relative has potentially died, we can't go in all guns blazing.'

Cathy shook her head sadly. 'No, and I hope he's all right.' A wave of guilt swept over her. James was so wise and understanding. What might have bothered him years ago, no longer did. He'd seen many doctors come and go and had accepted and dealt with all of their idiosyncrasies.

'Oh, sit down, Cathy, and talk,' her senior partner said abruptly.

Up until then, she had been standing propped against his sink top. Cathy looked at him in concern.

'Well, it's not really about Euan, is it? There's obviously something else.'

Cathy sat in the chair by his desk.

'Things running away with you again? I think we've all been a little lax at taking care of one another recently and I have noticed. I didn't want to jump in and say. I know you're quite capable of telling me if you have a concern. This last month or so... since you and Chris, well, I've been looking out. I've noted the extra hours you're working. Of course, you realise that it can't go on and you'll burn out. You're quite self-aware, far more so than most.' He looked at her, his brow furrowed. 'I don't want to make a fuss but if we can help at all, Cathy...'

'How will the place cope without you when you retire? How will I cope?'

He lapsed back in his chair with a sigh. 'I've put it off long enough. I was meant to be going nearly three years ago, but what with everything going on, well, it took a back seat.' He looked indulgently at her. 'Have you thought about putting the advert out? We, or rather, you, need to start making provisions. It took us long enough to replace poor Mark. You know how hard things were when it was just the two of us and Euan's not even full time. Why not ring up the deanery and see if there are any particularly good trainees coming through; or are you worried about age?'

Cathy grimaced.

'Yes, I see what you mean,' James said without her having to say. 'It would make you the senior partner and you're stressed enough as it is. It's not ideal, by any means. We should have planned better, Cathy. Euan seemed perfect at the time though, but someone with greater understanding...'

Cathy sighed. 'If someone with a bit more experience did come up, that would be better for me anyway. It's a concern, I'll admit. I'm aware that Euan has been like a breath of fresh air since he's started. I think the whole team feels it. Bar this minor transgression, he's been really good. He's fitted in quickly, he's popular with the staff and patients, and he's no shirker. He does his fair share and doesn't seem fazed by the responsibility.' Cathy rolled her eyes, knowing that what she was going to say was trivial. 'It's just a few minor things. I can't even put my finger on it, James. Just inexperience or naivety, I suppose. It's things you can't learn at medical school. As it happens, I heard something yesterday that was a bit concerning. I wanted to talk to Euan about it first. When I found out he had disappeared, I was a bit put out. It was important, you see? I wanted to clear the thing up.'

'Do you want to tell me? Does it impact on the practice at all?'

'Indirectly, I suppose. At a push, our reputation could be doubted. It's an out-of-hours matter really.' Cathy wavered, unsure if she should even discuss it without Euan there to explain his side to the story. Finally, she exhaled. James blinked slowly but didn't rush her or force her to speak. 'Oh, there's no big secret really,' she said. 'It sounds very much as if last week Euan was trying to be everyone's friend. He was finishing a shift for the evening. I think it was Dr Kidd taking over after him for the overnight shift. They had a late call, a chest pain, it seems. Remember, Euan was telling us about it the other day? It was out beyond the Ancrum Road. Well, I was at the out-of-hours base last night and I spoke to Dave Ramage, one of the drivers. He was singing Euan's praises. He thought he'd done the right thing. He said that it was a bit undecided who should go to the visit. By rights, it should have been Dave and Euan. The call came in on their shift, but they were never going to manage to drive there and back before clocking off time. If he'd been proactive, Dr Kidd might well have stepped up and said he'd take it instead, to save them finishing late. But, by the sounds of it, he didn't. I think Dr Kidd's been doing a lot of shifts. That, coupled with the fact that Dave's wife's in hospital, might have swayed it. Maybe the pair of them put a bit of pressure on Euan to do what he did.'

Cathy paused and smiled, aware that James was looking at her intently.

'No, honestly, it's not that bad really, but it is against out-of-hours protocol. He took the emergency drug bag, you see? He did the call in his own car, alone.'

When she had finished, the room seemed silent for a long time, although it must only have been a few seconds before James spoke. 'I see,' he said slowly as if tasting the words.

Cathy couldn't quite gauge what he thought. 'Do you know what I mean about being naïve now?' she asked. 'He put himself in quite a tricky position, potentially. If he had been accosted, if his car had been stopped, or if someone had known he was travelling alone, he could have been in a very vulnerable situation.'

James nodded but he remained tight-lipped. 'We'll discuss it when he returns,' he said.

Cathy wasn't sure if James was annoyed at her for being indiscreet. He seemed to be thinking the thing over still. She waited, unsure if she should get up and leave.

'I suppose, I should get on,' she finally said, shifting and pushing her chair back. 'I'm grateful for the chat and I promise I'll start advertising soon.' She got up and moved to the door.

'Cathy, before you go,' James said. 'You were looking into that odd case with the man and his missing wife. Did you get any further with that?'

'Not really,' she admitted, not wanting to tell him about the deserted house. 'Looks like they've moved anyway. I'm sure it was a false alarm, James. Just a mix-up on the husband's part. I did ask Linda, and she said that the wife had been having an affair before they even went out to India. I assume on returning, the woman took up where she'd left off, and Mr Steer has since cut and run. Linda said he was a bit of a business tycoon at one time. Used to be part of some pharmaceutical company. Goodness knows why he fell from grace.'

James slapped his hand down on his knee. The sound made her flinch. 'I knew the name rang a bell. Of course. I know exactly who you mean now. Adam Steer. He lives at old Balmuir House, the mansion. If only you'd said. That's going years back, I knew of the family though. His father was the tycoon, not him. He didn't have the brains. Bit of a playboy in his day, I seem to remember. How odd.' James chuckled. 'Steer, of course. I haven't heard of the family for a long time now. Not for years. I remember when I first started working here, I did a visit to the old man. The place was quite unbelievable,' James snorted. 'Cold though.'

Cathy was surprised. 'Really? Well, he wasn't living in the mansion anymore. He'd moved to the little lodge house on the mansion's estate. The big house belongs to someone else. The brother, I assume. He did mention a brother when he came into see me, right enough.'

James was shaking his head in recollection. 'My God. Years ago. That was the family home. One of the richest families in these parts. Owned all the land round about too,' he said, smiling with nostalgia. 'Bit of a sad end, of course. But these powerful people often sail close to the wind. Killed himself,' he said.

Cathy raised her eyebrows. 'Who?'

'Old Mr Steer. Hanged himself in that house, as it happens. Dreadful really. I think a story went around that he'd mismanaged the business in some way or other. No idea if it's true. As I say, he wasn't a regular patient of ours. Never showed any sign of depression or anything of that sort. Left the boys to tidy up his affairs between themselves. I've no idea how successful they were. Presumably, they managed if they still own that big old house.'

'Well, one of them was in the lodge, as I say.'

'Goodness knows why he's been living there. That would be some come down. You'd have thought if he'd lost the family fortune, the last thing he'd want to do was stay on just at the bottom of the drive. Memories would be dreadful. But like I say, I've not heard of any of the family in years. How strange he's popped up again.'

'Only to disappear just as quickly,' Cathy concluded rather tritely. 'But he'd been living in the area for a few years, James. Linda knew the wife vaguely through the gym.'

But James didn't seem to be listening. 'How strange,' he repeated shaking his head.

'I don't suppose there were grandchildren?' Cathy asked, suddenly remembering what she had heard as she stood outside the mansion house, eavesdropping.

'No idea. What makes you ask?'

'I thought someone mentioned a third generation, that's all, but maybe I misheard.'

James shook his head. 'Can't help you, Cathy.'

She left him to it and returned to her room. James was right. It was strange. Everything surrounding the Steer family seemed to grow more and more complicated and murky. A family with secrets, Cathy thought, but at least her conversation with James had given her an idea as to where she should next look for the missing couple. She would have to steel herself for the visit though. It wouldn't be pleasant, or easy.

11

I n the end, she found herself putting it off. She felt, for that
evening at least, she didn't have enough strength to go to the
mansion house and have a difficult conversation. Having
overheard whoever it was on that first night she had looked for
Mr Steer, she knew that the people who lived there were likely
to be unpleasant. She recalled the sneering words she had
heard. 'Bloody cat. She deserved what she got.' If they had been
talking about Mrs Steer, it didn't look good.

On the way home, she instead made a detour in quite the
opposite direction from Balmuir House. She would save that
dreaded visit for the morning. She had an admin session and
could fit it in at her leisure then. She would need to think hard
before going bulldozing in. What Linda had mentioned to her
earlier about Mrs Steer had played on her mind though, and she
had begun to wonder if there might be something useful gained
from investigating a different line of inquiry also. After all, if Mrs
Steer had a lover before going to India, might he not be in the
frame for her disappearance as well? Cathy could think of only
one place to find this out, but again, it would require some tact.

The nights were drawing in already, and despite it only

being six thirty, the sky had faded into the kind of half-light that makes driving harder than if it is pitch black. The town was busy, full of commuters wending their way back home. As she turned off from the high street, the street lights flicked on, indicating that it was officially evening. Everything took on an orange tinge.

A couple of children scurried across the road in front of her. Startled, Cathy braked hard, glancing then in her rear mirror to see that the car behind her had done so also. Thankfully they hadn't been too close or she might well have been shunted. The children seemed oblivious to the disorder caused and she put the car into first gear again and loosened her grip on the steering wheel. She looked right and saw the pair of them haring up a side street shrieking and laughing. For so long, it seemed she had felt this dull fatigue from responsibility. When had she last laughed, really laughed? The kind of childhood, side-aching, belly laugh that was ultimately so good for the soul. Cathy tried to think, but couldn't even remember.

As she slowly accelerated up past the line of shops; the pharmacy that so many of her patients used, and then the charity shop, she considered what she had learned about the unsettling situation so far. She had already heard a good deal about Mr Steer and his rather ambiguous fall from grace. If James was correct, the man had indeed been forced to change his outlook on life. Cathy couldn't imagine how it must have been growing up in such a privileged position. In many ways, it must have been wonderful having money and status of that kind. But with that, had come an expectation. Cathy knew that James had been shocked to hear about Mr Steer now only living in the small lodge house at the end of the drive. She had seen a look in his eyes. Perhaps in his long career, James had come into contact with others like Mr Steer. It was the age-old story of wealth not being enough. Who could say what Mr Steer had felt about the situation, but presumably being raised in the shadow of a successful father had, at the very least, spurred him on to hunt for accomplishment himself. He had been fruitful in his endeavours at one point anyway.

The wind had got up now, and it gusted just as she passed a side street. It buffeted the car, and Cathy clutched at the wheel. She was almost there. Goodness knows, she'd be glad enough to get home safely after this. She glanced in the mirror again and flicked on her right indicator and before turning, waited for the opposing line of traffic to clear.

Before her stood the old mill, a tall, impressive building, long since converted into executive flats. Alongside this was a plot that had once been farmed. Cathy remembered the area when she had arrived and how it had often suffered the ill effects of flooding from the nearby river. Since then, there had been a good deal of money ploughed into the town's flood defence system. A high wall had been built and the banks to the river better fortified. The value of the land since this development had increased considerably. But it had been worth far more to the owner as commercial real estate than agricultural land.

Cathy continued to mull her problem over as she waited for a gap in the traffic. As always, the car heater was on and the dry warm air caught at her throat making her cough. Tears sprung to her eyes and she hastily swatted them with the sleeve of her jacket.

She again considered Mr Steer's wife. How had Marjorie Steer fitted into the scene? Had she met her husband when he was on the up, or when he was coming down? What kind of a woman was she anyway? Cathy still knew so little about her. Having met Mr Steer, she at least felt that she had a grasp on his character. He had been bullish and proud. Impatient and, when she had spoken with him, easily irritated. Who then, was Mrs Steer?

Mr Steer had given her a few clues, she supposed. The way he had spoken about his wife, suggested that he held her in high regard. To come into the surgery that day, full of indignation and outrage, had surely not just revealed an impatience and bad temper. It seemed to Cathy, that the man had been gravely concerned for his wife. What else did she know from their conversation? Well, Marjorie Steer had been in India with him, that she knew. Despite what Linda had said about Mrs Steer's depression and dislike of her husband, Cathy couldn't reject the facts. The woman had, after all, tolerated her husband enough at the very least to go halfway around the world with him.

And this talk of domestic violence too, something had niggled about that. How could Mrs Steer possibly travel abroad, to a country she didn't know well, with no support network in place, if she was concerned for her safety? There lay the actual crux of the thing. In theory, Mrs Steer might easily have been disposed of while they were abroad if that was indeed what Mr Steer was meant to have done. Why on earth wait until they were back home, and then kick up a fuss about the woman's disappearance? No, it still made no sense at all. Cathy was inclined to believe that, at least at one point, the marriage had been a success.

But if the stories didn't align, whose version was to be believed? Had Mrs Steer exaggerated to Linda her dislike for her husband? She had been reported by several sources, including her husband, to have been having some sort of an affair at one point. Then, of course, was the evidence in the diary that the police had read. Mr Steer had dismissed it as feverish ramblings, but what if Mrs Steer had still been intent on meeting with her lover and leaving her husband behind? Affairs, Cathy supposed, happened more frequently than people cared to imagine. She hoped that she might be able to find out more about the man that Mrs Steer had been attracted to. Would he lead her to the missing couple?

The car park sprawled in front of her. The place was undoubtedly popular, and perhaps more so than Cathy had imagined it might be. She turned in and parked her car on the far side. Then, getting out, she fastened her jacket up against the bite of the wind and plunging her hands deep into her pockets, ran across the damp tarmac, splashing in the puddles as she did so. The industrial-sized building was illuminated and the logo painted in vivid, enthusiastic colours. Cathy remembered it being built. It had caused a bit of excitement as the town had never had a gym. The thing was a bit of an eyesore, to be honest, but it hadn't stopped the locals flocking. Cathy supposed that it had been a good thing for the community as a whole. Far too many patients she saw these days suffered from the complications of excess weight and immobility.

Cathy had not herself been tempted to sign up. As a student, she had been on the university running team and had burned off any excess stress or calories through that. It was years now since she had run. At one time, it had been quite a big part of her life and she had been reasonably good at the middle distances. Now, perhaps the solitude of pounding away the miles in silence frightened her.

She pushed the heavy revolving door and was met by a sudden rush of warm air from the heaters above. The foyer was bright. A couple of girls in matching tracksuit trousers and neon-green polo shirts were there. One of them pushed a frosted glass door leading from the foyer on the left. The thump of a bassline filled the entrance hall, and for a second or so, until the door swung back again, Cathy could hear laughter and the clink of metal on metal. She pictured a weight being dropped, and sweating gym-goers counting down the minutes until the workout was complete. The other girl dressed in neon-green smiled at her as she approached.

'Can I help?'

The desk in front of her was high, and Cathy propped an elbow on it, but it felt uncomfortable and she hastily allowed her arm to slip to her side.

'Oh, hello. Yes, I wonder if you can,' she said. Her stomach was beginning to churn. She glanced behind her and saw that another woman was now waiting. 'I wanted to see if anyone could talk to me about a friend of mine?'

The frosted door was opened again and the other neon-green polo shirt arrived and indicated that she would attend to the woman who had been waiting behind Cathy.

'What was the name?' the girl asked. 'We can't give out any information about clients. It's company policy.'

Cathy's heart sank. She hadn't realised that the gym would hold such high ethical standards. Perhaps this line of inquiry would get her nowhere after all. 'Marjorie Steer,' she said hopefully. 'I was meant to meet her here the other day and she didn't show. I wondered if she was booked in again later in the week. We usually run together.'

Cathy wasn't quite sure where all of this had come from, but now that she had begun the lie, she found her heart beating very fast indeed and she had to steady her arm on the desk in front to stop herself from visibly shaking.

'Oh, you're a member?' the girl asked. 'Sorry. I thought by the way you'd said it, you weren't with the gym. Your name?'

Cathy found herself announcing that she was 'Dr Linda Gauld.'

The girl nodded and typed this into the computer in front of her. 'Funny,' she said as she waited for the machine to do whatever it was that she was after. 'You'll not believe it, but when you walked in, I thought you were someone else.'

Cathy felt the blood drain from her face and she took a step back. Had the girl recognised her? She shouldn't have been so foolish as to expect to go incognito. She should have learned by now that being a doctor meant that she was recognised everywhere she went in the town.

The girl looked at her oddly and then smiled slightly. 'You'll think I'm mad,' she said, 'but for some reason, I thought you were from the police.'

Cathy laughed. 'Have they been in before then?'

The girl shot her a look and Cathy immediately regretted the remark. 'Why would they?'

Cathy shook her head and was silent once more.

'Ah yes,' the girl said, thankfully distracted by the words on the screen. 'Was it a class that you were both booked in for together? I'm looking but I can't see...'

'Not as such,' Cathy gabbled. 'My daughter had baby yoga and we got chatting in the foyer together. We agreed to go for a run after one of her sessions but she had said she might be going away for a while.'

The girl studied her computer. 'Not for...' she traced the entries on the screen with her finger. 'Not been in for the last ten weeks. Funny. She must have been away then. Her membership's coming up for renewal too. It says we've sent out reminders but she's not been in touch. Usually, a frequent attendee, going by this. She's been away, has she? Anywhere nice?'

Cathy now felt that the dynamic was all wrong. It had been her trying to find out answers, rather than the other way around. 'Listen, thanks anyway,' she said. 'I'll hopefully bump into her at some point in passing.'

Cathy backed away from the desk and began to move to the revolving doors. It had been stupid to come. Of course, no one would tell her anything. Why would they talk to her? She needed to get home. She was exhausted. As she reached for the glass panel though, she felt a hand on her back. The touch made her recoil.

'Wait just one minute.' The man's voice was sharp and Cathy froze.

At that moment, the bright lighting in the foyer was suddenly impossibly garish and she was too hot. Cathy's throat had become very dry. She swallowed but there was no saliva and she instead tasted metal. A fluttering panic filled her. She paused, afraid to turn. In her ears, she heard the thudding background drumbeat of the music in the gym but then she realised that it was the pulse of blood flowing in her ears and she wondered if she was going to faint. She had been found out, of course. Someone knew Linda and had overheard her pretending to be the other doctor.

As she turned, the brightness of the foyer seemed to drain. She held her car keys in her right hand. She had been fingering the cold metal in her pocket as she had spoken with the girl at the desk. Her fingers were numb now. She was acutely aware that she was being watched.

'The woman by the door,' someone said but the voice echoed and seemed distant.

It happened so gradually. The room fragmented before her. She even had time to turn slightly so that she might land on the mat by the door rather than the hard polished tiles.

Cathy didn't feel the keys slide from her hand but she heard the sharp chink as they landed just milliseconds before her head did the same.

Emptiness washed over her. It came like a thankful wave.

12

'Cathy. Cathy.'

The voice in her head was persistent and annoying. She frowned, preferring to drift where she was.

'Cathy, for goodness' sake, what have you been doing?'

The voice then spoke, presumably, to someone else. 'No, it's fine, I'm a doctor. It's a simple vasovagal. I know her. If you just give us some space. She'll come to, but better not have a thousand eyes on her when she does.'

Cathy's eyelids fluttered and she blinked. The man in front of her was familiar but she had one of those awkward moments, when you're sure you know someone, but can't place them. When it clicked, her face broke into a sheepish grin.

'Sorry, Stuart,' she faltered. 'It's because you're not in a suit.' Her mouth was tacky and her tongue stuck to her lips. 'What are the chances of your own GP being right there?' She laughed. She tried to say more, but she was slow and stupid.

'Cathy Moreland.' He laughed. 'What in the name of God's been going on?'

She was now lying at the side of the foyer. 'Jesus,' she said, suddenly realising what had happened. She tried to get up and the sudden rush of blood back to her face made her temples ache and her jaw tingle.

'Whoa,' he said. 'Just rest there a second.' He had been handed a polystyrene cup of water by someone, and he placed it in her hand, wrapping her fingers around it with his own. 'Sip,' he instructed. 'You're dehydrated.'

She drank awkwardly, spilling some of the ice-cold liquid down her jacket. 'I feel an idiot.'

'There you are. Better,' he said. 'No, we're fine now, thanks,' he told a concerned bystander. 'We'd better get you up if you've not bashed yourself too badly. I tried to grab you as you fell, but you lurched the other way. I sent someone to my car to grab my bag. Here they come.'

She got up slowly and supported by his arm, they made their way to a blue geometric sofa in the corner. He took his doctors' bag from a man wearing the neon green gym uniform.

'Cheers. Hopefully won't need it now, but thanks.'

All the same, he got out his pulse oximeter and placed it on her finger. She sat obediently, while he did his checks.

'Your pulse is very slow,' he said. 'Perhaps I should give you a low dose of something to bring that up.'

She sat meekly, her mind still a distorted mess while he rummaged in his bag. When she saw that he had produced a vial and a needle, she suddenly snapped.

'Hang on,' she said, shaking her head. 'I'm fine. I don't need anything, honestly. Just a sugar fix. Oh, my keys,' she said suddenly.

Dr Kidd put away his syringe and reached into his tracksuit trousers and produced the keys. 'I think five minutes before you drive though, at least, no? I'll grab a bar of chocolate. Your blood sugar's probably in your boots. Can you remember eating today?'

Not waiting for an answer, he crossed the foyer to a

dispensing machine. He was a tall athletic man and perhaps ten years older than Cathy. His hair had the kind of stippled grey to the tips that did not detract from his natural stylishness and only added to it. Cathy sipped her water, knowing that several of the staff were still watching her. What a fool she had made of herself.

'Badminton,' he said to her, returning with a bar of chocolate. 'That's why I'm here. I try every week, but I've been so busy. How are you, Cathy, anyway? I assume this is a one-off vasovagal episode? I didn't have you down as a gym bunny though.'

She snorted and peeled at the wrapper of the chocolate he had given her, but her fingers were cold and shaking, and she messed it up. All the time, he watched her levelly. She filled the silence, chattering far too quickly as she chewed.

'Well, you know I'm not that,' she said. 'As it happens, I used to do a bit of running, but not in a long time. Mainly 10Ks. I was quite good. On the uni team. How are you anyway, Stuart? All well up at Westfield?'

He ignored this. 'How are *you*, Cathy? Really?'

'I heard that Caroline's doing some of the academic stuff now. The rest of you'll be even busier because of it,' she babbled.

He smiled and sat down, perhaps accepting that the best way to deal with her was by being less direct. 'Yes, we're not twiddling our thumbs, by any means.' He laughed, glancing around and nodding to someone who looked on concerned. 'It only gets worse. And you? We've not had a joint learning afternoon between the practices in a while now. Need to sort that, I suppose. What's this I hear about James retiring, anyway? I thought the day would never come.'

Cathy had finished the chocolate and began to fold the wrapper. She rolled her eyes. 'I'm dreading James going if I'm honest. What with Mark dying and all the upheaval surrounding that, I'm not prepared to do without our senior partner. He's like an anchor, you know? God knows how the place will go on without him.'

'Are you going to look for a partner then? There's none out there, by the way. All the new kids are only interested in salaried posts and won't commit to a partnership. We're struggling for locums as it is. They charge anything. It seems like they make up a random figure and because we're so desperate, we end up forking out. It'll be the same for you, no doubt. The last one we had in, charged the same as the others but then when it came to divvying out visits, announced that he wasn't prepared to do them! Honestly, it's as bad as I've ever known it.'

By now, Cathy's heart rate had returned to almost normal and the hollow emptiness inside had subsided. 'Out of hours is much the same too,' she said, knowing that despite her recent embarrassment, she was leading the conversation in the direction she had wanted. 'I'm only doing the odd one or two. I heard you were doing your fair share though? One of the drivers said you're even covering overnights. I've no idea how you manage.'

'Nor do I.' He laughed. 'Money's good though. So, what were you asking about up at the desk just now anyway? I thought I overheard you saying you were looking for Linda, but that can't be right. I assume she's still with you guys?'

'Oh yes. Still with us, but no, Linda wouldn't be here at this time anyway. She clocks off bang on six o'clock to get home to pick up the kids. And there's no leeway.'

'Right.' He laughed. 'We've got a couple like that too. You know who I mean, of course. Even if an emergency's coming in, they'll dump it on those of us who have more grown-up families. Tricky, but then that's practices for you. You turn a blind eye to some of the smaller stuff and hope that everyone will pull together when it's needed. So, what are you doing here then if you're not going to pump some iron? You're welcome to join me with the badminton, but perhaps not tonight, I think, all things considered. Maybe save that for another day.'

Cathy looked disgusted at this suggestion. 'I hardly think so,' she said and then laughed. 'No, I was just seeing if one of our patients had been in actually. She's gone AWOL and I had heard that she was a member. It doesn't matter. I was just passing and it was a spur of the moment thing. I should be getting home myself.' She began to get up.

'You're still free on Wednesday mornings, are you? Isn't it set aside for paperwork?'

Cathy shot him a look.

'I think you're due to come in for a chat soon,' he continued smoothly. 'Just pick a time, Cathy and the girls will make a space for you. I'll see you whenever suits.'

She was standing now. The room felt level and the ground didn't wobble.

'Don't leave it any longer than a week,' he said, now getting up also. 'If I don't hear from you, I'll be calling on you. I hope tonight was a one-off episode and you're looking after yourself.'

Their eyes met once more. Cathy had been seeing him professionally for just over two years now and he had been a great support to her following her return to work. It had been a recommendation made by her psychiatrist. He advised that she must clock in with her own GP at least every couple of months so that her medication could be checked and her mood assessed. It was all very well being a GP herself, but ultimately, Cathy couldn't have a detached viewpoint. Without a doctor outwith her own practice seeing her, she might easily slip into a hypomanic state once more, and with little warning. Although now the arrangement with Dr Kidd was quite routine, she still found the dynamic hard to swallow. Being a sick doctor was one of the most unbearable experiences.

She left him and made her way across the car park. The moon was now visible and the evening was growing cold. When she had arrived, there had still been some light in the sky. The rainy blues and greys had since turned to a thousand shades of black. The overhead lights in the car park cast warped shadows across the asphalt and familiar shapes of cars and trees took on an ominous ambiguity.

The clock on her dashboard said that it was gone seven thirty. She would head home and get an early night. She was thoroughly ashamed of what had happened at the gym. Fainting, and in front of not only all of those people but one of her colleagues and her own GP. How humiliating.

She started the car and pulled out to join the line of traffic. Within metres, she was at a standstill due to the red traffic light. It was only a chance glance back that led her to notice and when she did, she felt quite sick. A car was slowly turning. She watched, at first disinterested. Only as it moved around, she saw the familiar faulty tail light. With a sinking feeling, she knew that she was being followed. Someone, for some reason, was watching her.

13

When Cathy awoke, she lay blinking and disorientated. She had had a nightmare about being chased and the bedcovers were in disarray. There was a strange heaviness upon her, like a great weight on her chest. She had to fight off the thickness of sleep to realise why; and when she did her situation came flooding back with sickening clarity. She shifted and coughed twice. The spasms made her ribs ache and she lay back again, exhausted on the white pillows.

Slowly, she allowed the events of the previous week to infiltrate her consciousness. Her eyes fluttered as she remembered it all. The initial visit from Mr Steer now seemed like a lifetime ago. What had become of him and his wife? And who had been responsible for obliterating every trace of their existence? She thought of the previous night and the car with the faulty tail light. It had shaken her a good deal. When she had arrived home to the empty house, she had immediately locked the front door and rather than heading straight for the kettle and radiators, she had gone around the house, checking the other doors and windows were also inaccessible.

Her day ahead filled her with misgiving. She knew that she

must go up to Balmuir House. She had put it off quite long enough. It had been the Steer's family home, after all, and perhaps the people now living there might hold the key to the mystery. Having already met one of them however, she felt sure that the encounter today would be awkward. She recalled the man's haughty manner and dismissive way of dealing with her that night she had stood outside the lodge house. And then there was the strange conversation she had overheard outside.

Gradually, she began to get up. Her limbs felt heavy like they didn't want to do what she asked. She was exhausted, as if the fog of sleep still had not left the edges of her mind. She forced her legs over the side of the bed. The cold air on her feet made her shrink. She shivered and forced herself to continue, placing her feet on the ground and testing to see how steady she was. The room felt uneven, but she slowly moved to the bedroom door. She must surely have caught a bad head cold. That, coupled with her forgetting to eat, must have made her faint the previous night and it was causing her to feel shaky still.

She showered, leaning at times on the glass panel. The steam filled her nostrils and as it fogged the room around her, her mind slowly cleared. She had no reason to be so jumpy and on edge. All she was doing was looking into a concern she had over a missing patient. She was entirely within her rights to do so. She was a clinician and her duty of care to her patients did not simply stop when they left her consulting room.

The bedroom felt impossibly cold despite the shower. She quickly found a smart pair of trousers and rummaged in her drawer for the warmest jumper she could find. She found a reasonable one bundled in at the back and hastily pulled it over her damp hair. It felt like a fleecy hug, and she smoothed the folds of wool around her. She glanced instinctively at her dresser. She had read Chris's note countless times over. She knew the words by heart. Not today.

Cathy looked in the mirror and smiled at her reflection. Her pale countenance stared back. Perhaps she was anaemic after all. She must check her blood results. Although she had been reluctant at first when Euan mentioned it, she had asked for James to do the favour all the same.

'James,' she had said, tapping on her senior partner's door that morning.

He looked up from his desk, and closed the case notes he had been studying. 'Cathy. How's the morning? Cracking on with insurance claims?'

Cathy grimaced. It was an ongoing battle to try and get on top of all of the letters and forms that needed to be dealt with daily. The insurance claims were the greatest issue and had been for some time. The pile requiring the doctors' attention never seemed to recede, even when one of them made a committed effort to tackle it.

'Never-ending,' she sighed. 'James, I don't suppose you'd heard from Euan at all? I assumed he would be in touch.'

'I should have said. It slipped my mind,' he confessed. 'Sorry, Cathy, I meant to say. His grandmother died. He's staying in Dublin to organise the funeral. I'm sorry I didn't mention it first thing. Said he'd be back on Monday. I told him to take as long as he needed, of course.'

'Did he ring you directly, then?'

'Not my mobile, no. He called the practice. The girls put him through to me. I could tell he was in a rush so there wasn't much said. He was apologetic, as you can imagine.'

Cathy nodded. 'Yes. I see. Listen, James, I was going to ask. I've been hunting through blood results today, and I can't find my own ones. Remember you did them as a favour the other day?'

James began to move paper around his desk, lifting case notes and putting them down again. 'They didn't go on the computer of course because you're not a registered patient here,' he said. 'I was looking at them earlier. Can't find it... Hang on, Cathy, I can't see where they've gone. They were normal though. You're not anaemic, although I still think you could do with a hearty meal and a holiday!'

Cathy smiled. 'Don't bother to find them. That's fine. Listen, I'm about to head out to do a quick call. Everything under control for now?'

James leaned back in his chair. 'Nothing outstanding and plenty of appointments left for the afternoon. I've got it covered. If you've anything you need to get done while you're out, don't rush back.'

Cathy paused and looked at her partner quizzically.

'Appointments, for example,' he continued, looking somewhat guiltily up at her. 'Maybe today would be a good day to call and make one...'

'What, you heard already? But how?' And then in sudden realisation. 'You've got to be kidding,' she said angrily.

'Don't jump the gun,' James said, holding his hands up. 'It was well-meant.'

'And he called you when? This morning? God, nothing's a bloody secret for long. It was a vasovagal. I was tired and hadn't managed to grab lunch.' She didn't wait for his reply. 'James, that's out of order, surely you can see.'

'Cathy, will you sit down and stop overreacting? It's not out of order at all, as it happens. You know that Dr Kidd has your best interests at heart. He's a damn good doctor and a good friend to you. If you'd like to recall, as GPs, we have a duty of care to our patients. That includes taking care of our own health. Imagine how I felt hearing that you'd collapsed last night. Stuart was quite concerned. You know I shouldn't be taking your bloods and doing these informal consultations. I'm too close to you and it's unethical. Stuart is your GP.'

Cathy frowned.

'Quite apart from the physical side of things, your mental stability needs to be assessed as a matter of routine. It's just the way it is. Now, when I retire, you're going to have to take a firmer hold of yourself and you'll need someone else keeping half an eye on you. Now's not the time to discuss it but I had wondered about Linda. She's spoken to me quite recently about being worried about you.'

'She did what? Now you and Linda have been discussing my mental health, have you? Since when, James? I honestly can't believe it of you!'

'She cares, Cathy. We all do. You'll run yourself into the ground at this rate. It's no good and it's not sustainable. You're a fine doctor. You're dedicated and you care, sometimes too much. This has to stop though. You're in a downward spiral and I'm genuinely worried as if I haven't enough to think about,' he finished to himself.

Her hand was on the door handle. 'You've no need,' she said. 'Soon you'll be retired and we'll have found someone better anyway.'

As she slammed the door, she felt sick at what she had just said. She loved and respected James. Their relationship went much deeper than clinicians working side-by-side. She recalled suddenly her friend Suzalinna's words just after Chris had left. 'You always wound the ones you love the most. It's human nature,' Suzalinna had said.

Cathy continued to think of this as she drove from the practice, turning up the long road, but she forgot it almost as soon as the high metal gates came into her line of sight on the left-hand side. Cathy signalled and drove up the gravelled drive, passing the now-empty lodge house on the right where Mr and Mrs Steer had once lived. The tall trees, half-bare from the ravages of wind and cold, lined the driveway. Despite the stark morning light, the approach to the house felt oppressive and shadowy.

The drive snaked upwards and the house came into view properly. A vast building, divided by tall, high windows. Cathy felt her mouth dry. She took it all in, the creeping ivy that climbed the ancient walls. It seemed to assault the place completely and without check. Cathy had read once that although it might look appealing, vines of this sort could ruin the integrity of a house. If allowed to, they ran rampant, like a malignancy, gnawing away at the healthy brickwork and causing it to crumble to dust.

She parked her car and with the engine off sat for a moment in silence. The wind had begun to get up and a sudden gust made the car judder. Cathy bit her lip. It was now or never. Steeling herself, she unclicked her seat belt and opened the car door, holding on to it tightly lest it caught. The wind seemed to encircle her. It filled her ears and made her eyes stream. Cathy shivered as she walked up the stone steps that led to Balmuir house. She felt sure that a place such as this must hold some secrets, but were they the ones she sought to expose?

14

The grey-haired woman, who Cathy assumed was the housekeeper, led the way through the tiled vestibule, her heels clicking as she went. The echoes ricocheted back from the vaulted ceiling, making Cathy jump.

The staircase was carpeted in a deep red and swept majestically to the upper floors. All around the wood-panelled hall hung pictures in gilt frames. Cathy paused to look above at a portrait on the right. A vaguely familiar-looking gentleman scowled down at her. His grey eyebrows were heavy and his mouth, thin. Cathy felt like she had been reprimanded for something. Overhead hung a great chandelier. Although it was not lit, the sun from the upstairs windows touched the glass, sending slivers of brightness across the mahogany. As she glanced around her, Cathy couldn't help wondering where old Mr Steer had ended his life. What a terrible discovery for the person who'd found him and how desperate he must have been to do such a thing.

The woman opened a door to the side of the hall. Cathy saw that her hands were a deep mottled red. She wondered if the woman she had assumed was housekeeper to the mansion had contact dermatitis, a form of eczema common in people often handling cleaning products. But walking through, Cathy felt that the other woman didn't have the appearance of someone who would regularly get on their hands and knees to scrub anyone's floor.

'You'll wait in here,' the elderly woman said. Her voice was dry and cracked. It seemed more of a demand than a request.

Cathy quickened her steps, finding her footfalls too heavy and loud. She nodded to the woman as she passed. Before she could say anything though, the door was closed behind her and she stood alone, unsure now what to expect.

She had said that she only wanted a brief word with the owner of the house, and when asked her name, Cathy had said she was Dr Moreland from the Glainkirk Practice. She had no idea quite how this information would be received but when the woman had suggested she should come inside and wait, she had done so.

She turned now from the closed door and looked about the room. It was equally grand but what once might have been a jewel-coloured carpet was now quite dull and threadbare. The fireplace was laid but the dust on the logs indicated that this offering was merely for show. Cathy doubted that a roaring fire ever welcomed any guests.

She stood for some minutes listening, not daring to move for fear of someone coming, but as time passed, she became more daring and she crept across the hearth rug to take a better look at the photographs on the mantelpiece. One was of a beautiful man, perhaps in his thirties. The photograph was black and white and Cathy guessed it had been taken perhaps in the sixties, with the man lounging against a sports car, in wide-legged suit trousers and a shirt unbuttoned a couple of holes too low. He seemed fully aware of his magnetism and was beaming at the photographer. His perfect teeth were a stark contrast to his tanned skin. Almost forgetting where she was, Cathy found her mouth twitching into something of a smile. Her flirtation with the picture was abruptly cut short though as the door to the room was suddenly opened and a tall man came in.

The whole thing might have been comical had it not been so awkward. They stood looking at one another for what seemed an eternity. Cathy's heart was racing and she felt sick. He looked her up and down slowly as if appraising her. She felt the blood rush to her face and she swallowed a couple of times.

In truth, the man who had flung the door open so abruptly was somewhat of a relief to her. She had expected the angry-looking man from in the car the other night. But instead of dark scowling features, she found that this man was of fair complexion with honey-dark hair. He was slightly ruffled and windswept as if he had just come from outside. Despite the distance, his eyes were a striking blue and his mouth held a knowing smirk, as if there was a joke only he was party to.

When he finally spoke, it was with the drawl of private education. 'Mrs Sturrock said we had a visitor, but I had no idea...'

Cathy, who had thus far been frozen to the spot, stepped forward inelegantly, half stumbling as she did so. 'I'm Dr Moreland. I'm afraid I'm troubling you at an awkward time.'

'Delighted.' He laughed. 'Mrs Sturrock might have offered you a drink. She's been with us for bloody years and she always is a little odd with strangers. Territorial, if you ask me,' he said, allowing his voice to drop to a conspiratorial whisper.

He lounged forward to take her hand. His fingers were cool and he held onto her hand for a second too long. When he released her, she shivered, letting her hand slip again to her side.

'A house call?' he asked in an offhand manner, stepping away.

Without warning, he swung suddenly around. Cathy was

startled and staggered back in fear, her heart hammering in her chest. He paused a moment and looked quizzically at her, before slowly peeling his overcoat from his shoulders and draping it over the arm of a chair.

'You're jumpy, aren't you?'

Cathy attempted to keep her voice level. 'I'm sorry to trespass on your time, but I had been hoping to speak to someone who was in residence regularly. At least, that is to say...' She glanced sideways at his expression. He was now perched on the back of a chair and had folded his arms. He looked at her in mild amusement but was making a show of giving her his undivided attention.

'What I mean to say is,' she continued, 'I was hoping to speak to someone who had been here, staying here last week and possibly the week before even. It's about the lodge at the entrance gates. I'd hoped to find out if anyone had noticed anything odd.'

He shifted. 'And for what reason, might I ask, Doctor...?'

'Doctor Moreland. Cathy. It was a patient of mine. A Mr Steer. Adam Steer. I'm rather concerned for him, I'm afraid.'

Cathy was sure she had caught a glimpse of emotion crossing the man's face as she mentioned Mr Steer's name, but if she had, it was only momentary and he was once again relaxed and easy in his manner. 'Well,' he said, in a satisfied tone. 'And I thought our national health service had gone to the dogs. I am wholly impressed though if these are the lengths to which our rural practitioners are now going.'

Cathy's heart was beating hard in her ears. She tried to hide the tremor in her voice when she spoke. 'I'm sure it might sound amusing, but it's rather urgent, as it happens. I'm very much afraid that something has happened to Mr Steer, not to mention his wife. Seeing as they lived, at least at one time, at the bottom of your garden, I wonder if you could help me.'

The man grinned. The smile, although younger, was the same as the one in the black and white photograph. 'I like you, Cathy,' he confessed. 'Tell me what you want to know and I'll try my best to help. I live here. It is my family home.'

The next half hour was a blur. It seemed that her slightly audacious words had had some impact, and the man, who finally introduced himself as Archie, plumped a cushion on the chair across from him and indicated that she should take a seat.

'Sorry,' he said, 'I was being a buffoon. I've inherited that trait from my father.' He pointed to the photograph that she had been studying when he came in. 'Cathy, should we get Mrs Sturrock to run and make us a tea? You look frozen to death. No? Well, tell me, what's the story? You're quite worried, aren't you?'

She sat on the edge of a high-backed armchair and clasped her hands tightly in her lap. 'I am worried, yes. Mr Steer came to me last week. He was in a bit of a state, if I'm honest. He and his wife had returned from India just recently. She'd not been well on the night of her return though.' Cathy stopped. Realising that perhaps she was saying too much, and afraid of breaching confidentiality, she looked at her hands. 'Sorry,' she said. 'Are you... I mean, can you tell me about the circumstances of them taking on the lodge house?'

'It's not a bad little house,' Archie said as if considering it for the first time. 'I imagine they might have been quite comfortable there. But, if I'm honest, I'm not surprised they've cut and run. The arrangement wasn't going to be a long-term solution. It never could have been.'

'I don't want to pry...' Cathy began and he laughed a little cruelly.

'No, of course, you don't. Families, eh? Are you married, Cathy? Have any children?'

Cathy shook her head.

'No. I didn't think so,' he said, turning his gaze to the window and the windswept expanse of lawn. 'You must surely be quite a catch though, with a medical degree and successful career.'

She shifted awkwardly but didn't speak.

'Does it put them off?' he asked, returning to his former arrogance. 'Intelligence? Self-sufficiency? It must be hard to know who to trust. Everyone wants a piece of you. Perhaps we're not that different, in that respect. I know my wife was an unashamed gold digger. Oh, don't get me wrong,' he said hastily. 'I was aware of it from the start. It's not as if it suddenly dawned upon me. I got what I wanted and she did too. Divorced now,' he concluded. He studied her. 'You'd go for another doctor though, surely. They'd understand the pressures of the job. They'd know you inside and out.'

Cathy went to speak but he turned his head away from her and continued. 'Adam, I think, may have landed up in the same boat as me. He never did have any insight though. Bumbled around with his head in the clouds. It was always the same. Eddie and I had the brains. What a family.'

'Adam, Eddie...?'

The man gave her the broadest of smiles. His teeth were so perfect and even and had it not been for the spiteful twist to his mouth, he would have been impossibly handsome. 'The man you keep referring to as Mr Steer is my brother, Adam. I suppose I do know him better than most.'

There was a dreadful silence.

'I don't understand about the lodge house and about him leaving,' she began, but she could see that the mood had changed considerably.

'Cathy,' he said seriously. 'I think it best for everyone concerned if you stop this.' He smiled broadly at the ceiling and Cathy wondered if he was about to laugh. Instead, he turned back to her. 'Eddie and I spent half of our lives scurrying around trying to make things right. Adam, on the other hand...' When he spoke again, he almost spat the words at her. 'Well, you met him. You surely saw what he is. Goodness knows why father was blind to it. Like I said, he got his comeuppance the day he married that woman. She played him for the fool he was and good on her, I say. I know Eddie feels the same. We all do.' His leg bobbed back and forward. Cathy looked at his expensive, brown polished shoes. The right one lifted and fell, up and down, showing a patch of faded sole.

Without realising, she must have shaken her head in disbelief.

'No?' he asked. 'What would you know, anyway? Listen to me, Dr Moreland. You've done your duty. You've completed your little background check on your precious patient. It seems to me it was more of a gossip-dredging exercise than anything else though. Adam's gone. We can only hope he'll not be back. I think you can put this little case of yours to bed and concentrate on more deserving individuals. My brother was certainly never one.'

His eyes were an icy blue and his mouth set hard. Cathy found that she was trembling. From somewhere within, she found strength though, and with that, came anger. How dare he frighten her like this when all she was doing was the very best for a patient?

'Your tone is aggressive,' she stated. 'I'm no scandalmonger. I've no interest in your family's troubles whatsoever. I know something's not right and I won't be fobbed off.'

She got up stiffly and walked to the door. Opening it, she turned with her hand still on the handle. 'I'm sorry I offended you. I'll not trouble you again.'

15

She stumbled out of Balmuir House and into her car and hysterically looking around her, saw two dark saloons parked around the side of the building. In a rush of panic, she wondered who else besides Archie had been in the house all that time. She faltered opening the driver's door and for some reason, the key fob hadn't been working as it should. When she eventually got in, she was in such a state, she tried to accelerate but instead, stalled and came to a convulsive halt, sending gravel spraying up the sides of her wheels. She had heard James's voice in her head. 'You're going to have to start taking a firmer hold of yourself.' Cathy took a breath and turned the key again. She put her car in first and slowly released the clutch. Yes, perhaps James had been right, but he had done her an injustice in speaking about her health to Linda. That, she just could not let go.

She drove back to the practice in a dream-like state and getting out of her car, stumbled, dropping her keys in a puddle.

She bent and scrabbled in the greasy water, retrieving them and wiping them on her jacket. She walked into the practice and nodded to Michelle who was sitting behind the front desk. The receptionist was in conversation with an elderly man. He was pointing a finger and talking animatedly. Michelle raised her eyebrows and smiled as she passed.

James's door was closed and she felt a rush of relief. It was ridiculous really. She needed to apologise for how she had left things, but after what she had just been through, she didn't feel strong enough.

Cathy sat at her desk now and checked her computer. The girls had filled her messages with several medication requests and a couple of telephone consultations. Cathy sighed. What a mess she had made of things that day. She reran the excruciating conversation with the man she now knew to be Archie Steer. What a strange individual he was and how odd that she had not heard of him before, or his other brother, Eddie.

She thought of the night she had stood outside the mansion house hoping to ask after Mr Steer, but instead, she had heard the two men, presumably Archie and Eddie, talking about a woman. 'Bloody cat,' they had called her. If it had been Mrs Steer they meant, it didn't look good. But there was another phrase that had played on her mind since she had heard it that night also. 'Third generation...' What did that mean? Was there a chance that Mrs Steer had been pregnant? Would this child potentially inherit the family fortune? Of course, the baby would have to be Mr Steer's and not her lover's. Would someone be willing to abduct and kill, to prevent Mrs Steer from continuing the pregnancy? Were the Steer brothers capable of such a crime? She wondered if either was known to the practice.

Delaying her waiting medication requests and phone calls, Cathy keyed in the name. Nothing came up. She retyped: Archibald instead of Archie, but still, no match. In fact, nothing was coming up under 'A. Steer' at all. Cathy flopped back in her chair and then, in sudden realisation, sat up again. How could there be no 'A. Steer' when only last week she had seen Adam Steer, the man's brother?

With growing confusion, Cathy typed in Adam's full name. Nothing.

'Where is he?' she said aloud.

Cathy scrolled back through her calendar of appointments. With her heart hammering now she located the correct day. She knew almost before she arrived at the appointment in question, what she would find. It was with a sickening feeling that she saw the consultation slot when she had most definitely seen Mr Steer, was now completely blank.

Cathy looked around her room in a kind of wild panic. She felt as if someone was deliberately trying to confuse her.

'I saw him. I did. Where is he?'

Getting up, she went to the door and flung it open. James was coming slowly towards her with a patient. He saw her but looked away. Cathy wanted to shout out at him, but he was opening the door to his room and ushering the woman inside. The door closed behind. Cathy looked up and down the corridor again. She could hear Linda's voice. She was talking in a cheerful, reassuring manner to someone. Her door must have been left ajar for Cathy to be able to catch the odd word. She needed to speak to someone.

How could someone disappear from the computer system? And who had been responsible for erasing the case notes?

Knowing that she must pass through the waiting room, Cathy tried to compose herself. Her head ached and her breathing was shallow. She swallowed a couple of times and smoothed the creases from her trousers. Then, feeling as if all eyes were on her, she crossed the corridor and walked to the front desk.

Michelle was just finishing a telephone call. She had her headphones on and she moved the foam microphone a little away from her mouth. Beside her was Gill, one of the newer receptionists. Gill looked up at Cathy and smiled thinly.

'Dr Moreland. What can we do for you?'

'It's Michelle I need actually, but thanks, Gill. All okay?'

'Quiet now,' Gill said.

Cathy stood and drummed the tips of her fingernails on the countertop. Gill, probably guessing that there was a problem, picked up a random piece of paper and disappeared through to the back room. When Michelle pressed the button on her phone to end the call, she too must have understood. She took her headset off.

'Dr Moreland?'

'I need to talk to you. Get someone back on reception and come through to my room now.' Cathy spun and left the poor girl in no doubt that there was trouble brewing.

Michelle followed a minute or so later. She came into Cathy's room tentatively.

'Close it behind you,' Cathy said, from where she stood by the window. The receptionist did as she was told, clearly ill at ease with her employer's manner.

Cathy struggled to find the words at first and when she did, she couldn't help but vent some of the frustration that she felt.

'Michelle, sit down. Can you explain to me how a patient's records, someone I had seen only a week or so ago, would suddenly disappear?'

Michelle looked confused. 'What, the hard copy? They might be in the trays for dictation. Gill was going through a number of...'

Cathy held up her hand. 'Not hard copies. The computer records.'

Michelle shook her head.

'Explain to me how they, in their entirety, could suddenly vanish from our database.'

'I don't understand,' Michelle said. 'If you give me the name, I'll try and...'

'Go on then. Do it now, in front of me. Find the notes.'

Michelle got up and edged around the desk. She sat down in Cathy's chair and clicked on a different icon. 'I'll try through my office account, rather than yours,' Michelle said, glancing sideways. 'Maybe it's an issue with the doctors' accounts. What name?'

Cathy told her and watched as the girl typed it in. Nothing. Cathy leaned over and moved her aside. 'Hang on a minute,' she said and from where she stood, frantically typed in 'Marjorie Steer'. Once again, the computer cited 'invalid name'. Cathy stepped back and throwing her hands up in the air, cursed.

'Michelle, don't you remember Mr Steer coming in last week? Not a pleasant man. Impatient and demanded to see me, or any of the doctors that morning as a matter of urgency. I fitted him in. Tall, dark.'

'I don't... I mean I believe you, of course, but we see so many people every day and half of them are rude and obnoxious.'

But Cathy was now pacing the room and hadn't even heard what she said. 'Something's going on. Something's very wrong here. You can't just delete a patient's notes off the system. Even our dead patients stay on for a few weeks until the physical notes are returned to the Health Board. How could it be done? And not just to one, but two. Him and his wife. It doesn't make sense.'

'Has your patient transferred to another practice, Dr Moreland? Did he mention a move? I can't remember any notes going through this week, but perhaps...'

Cathy shook her head vehemently. 'He wasn't moving. He'd only just come back. All the time he was away in India his notes were on our system. Why did they go now?'

'I'm sorry...' Michelle began, obviously unsure what to

suggest. 'I promise I didn't do anything to the computers. None of the girls did.'

Cathy sighed. She suddenly felt quite defeated. 'No, no. I realise that, Michelle. I'm sorry to frighten you. It just doesn't make a bit of sense to me.' Something then occurred to her. 'Has anyone been into the practice from the Health Board recently? Anyone checking our files?'

'No, nothing like that. The computer maintenance people were in doing Dr Duncan's computer while he's been away. I think the man said that the department had had a complaint about some issue with some of the computers needing to be rebooted halfway through the day, or something. It didn't disrupt anything because of the room being free anyway. I showed him through and he was finished within the hour. Nice chap.'

'What did he look like?' Cathy knew that she sounded desperate.

Michelle considered. 'Darkish, good-looking enough. I don't know what to say.'

'Didn't he have any distinguishing features?'

Michelle shook her head. 'He was shut away through in Dr Duncan's room, so we didn't see much of him. If I can do anything else,' she said, but Cathy shook her head.

'It might just be a case of waiting until tomorrow,' Michelle said. 'I can't understand how it doesn't happen more often. All that information and none of it ever goes astray. Maybe leave it until the afternoon even, and check again. It might have popped back on the system again.'

Cathy smiled her thanks but knew that the files for Mr and Mrs Steer would not miraculously reappear again. They were lost, along with the people themselves.

16

It was late in the evening by the time Cathy got home. Despite realising now that the Steer family secrets were far more sinister than she might have imagined, Cathy found herself distracted that afternoon. She still had work to do, and no matter how worrying the case had become, she must see to that first. In many ways, it was as well. It felt good to be immersed in something she was comfortable with. Her job was, on so many levels, her calling. It was who she was and even after a hectic day, or week, she never doubted her reasons for becoming a doctor.

That afternoon, she had a list of patients to see and some minor surgery cases booked in also. She rather enjoyed the variety that her minor surgery list gave her. A good number were contraceptive implants or coils. She also attended to skin lesion removals. As the afternoon progressed though, and she was forced to leave the minor surgery room to collect a set of notes, her and James's paths crossed. Cathy became acutely aware of James's distance, his lack of eye contact and his hurriedly retreating figure. It pained her to have caused the rift, but being headstrong, she found it hard to apologise.

Her last patient of the day was a man with an altered naevus. It certainly required excision and pathology investigation. As she slowly removed the mole, running a perfect line around it, leaving wide margins in case it did turn out to be cancerous, she allowed her mind to return to that dreadful morning and the strange encounter with Archie Steer. What an odd man he had been, and what could he possibly have to hide unless he was implicated in his brother's disappearance? And then there were the computer records.

Had the Steer family been instrumental somehow in arranging for the case histories to be deleted off the computer system? Cathy thought about how Michelle had described the man who had come into the practice with the excuse of fixing a computer issue. Had it been Archie's brother, Eddie, the same dark-featured man she had herself met once on the drive up to Balmuir House? It all seemed so far-fetched though and she felt foolish even to consider such a thing.

Having carefully stitched and dressed the man's wound, Cathy peeled off her latex gloves and tidied away her minor surgery kit while her patient got dressed. Cathy depressed the bin pedal with her boot and dropped the gloves in.

'Take your time getting up, Mr Hayes,' she said, rubbing the creases from her trousers.

She paused and waited for him to dress. As she stood by the side of the room, she caught sight of herself in the mirror. Her face was pale and this was only highlighted further by the overhead lighting in the room. The shadows beneath her eyes looked like deep bruises, and her cheekbones seemed sharp and fragile. Cathy blinked, finding her reflection painful. Her hair had been cut a month or so ago. She had asked them to make it short so that she wouldn't need to spend so long washing and styling it in the morning. It had been a bit of a treat to herself. An impulsive decision at a far too expensive hair salon. Usually, she wouldn't have splashed out, but the pick-me-up was meant to boost her mood. Like so many women before her, she had thought that changing her image might bring closure to a relationship and moving forward, she might enjoy the confidence a new style might give her. When she had left the place her hair had been a glossy bob. But the effect the makeover might have had on her had been short-lived. Now, with the lank strands falling across her cheeks, she barely recognised herself.

Her patient had asked her something and Cathy turned and smiled an apology. 'Sorry,' she said. 'Are you all right there? No, the stitches will only need checking with the nurse next week. I'll not need to see you unless there are any issues but I will see you when the results are back. I'm not expecting anything troublesome though, as we discussed.'

The man gathered his jacket and with thanks, left. And then Cathy was once again alone. She found herself going through the surgical sets and checking that an order had been put in for more equipment. Then, she returned to her consulting room and checked off the late blood results. She heard James's light being switched off, and his footsteps up the corridor. She held her breath, wondering if her senior partner might tap on the door as he passed, but the footfalls didn't hesitate and he continued. Cathy sighed heavily. She was a fool. She should have patched things up with James. She would worry about the thing all night now until the following day.

She sat alone, as afternoon turned to evening, working her way through the laboratory results, keeping her mind busy, signing the last of the prescription requests that had come for the doctors to check at the end of the day. She heard doors being closed and Linda's voice as she said goodnight to one of the nurses further down the corridor. Still, Cathy sat hunched at her desk. As her room grew darker, the lights of cars turning in the car park outside glanced in through her window, their beams sending shafts of brilliant illumination over the room. When the sound of the last car dissipated into the background drone of commuters in the distance going home, she could barely distinguish it. Still, she sat.

The radiator behind her clunked twice: the heating was always set to go off at the end of the day. The sudden closeness of the noise made her grimace. She slowly stretched her arms above her head. When she did move, she realised that her shoulders and neck ached. It was time to go home. She had finished all of her paperwork and it couldn't be put off any longer.

She logged off and closed down her computer before collecting her jacket and bag. She found herself hesitating in the doorway and glancing around the room. What she looked for; she did not know. Then decisively, she flicked the lights and pulled the door to, locking it behind. The corridor was still lit and she walked to the back door, hearing only her footfalls. The rest of the building was completely silent. As far as she knew, all the clinicians had left. Their handyman, Bert, was usually the last to go, and so she rarely set the alarm or turned off the lights. She stood by the back door listening, and then, hearing a slight noise from where she had come, she called out.

'Bert? Can I leave you to set the alarm?' Her voice sounded hollow.

No answer came. All she heard was the thud of her blood in her ears.

Already feeling jittery, Cathy shook her head in self-disgust. Was she alone in the building, or not? Becoming annoyed with herself, Cathy firmly retraced her steps along the corridor. She touched each of the doors in turn, but all were locked. The place seemed somehow different at night. Although the corridor lights still gave a garish clarity to the place, she found herself misjudging quite ordinary objects. The first chair in the waiting room had looked as if someone was crouching. She did a double-take and clutched at her throat. Snorting at her stupidity, she continued past the waiting area to reception.

'Hello,' she called. 'Michelle? Bert? Is anyone still about before I leave and set the alarm?'

She froze as the door to the backroom unexpectedly clicked behind her. Cathy spun around, imagining she had seen a shadow move, but it had been her own, of course. How silly she was being. Everyone had left and she would set the alarm and leave. She hurriedly retraced her steps, no longer chastising herself for her growing panic, but wanting nothing more than to be safely in her car. In the end, she jogged the last few strides, reaching out to the cold metal of the fire escape handle and depressing it. But she was forgetting the alarm. Reluctantly, having come so close to freedom, she released the handle and turned to the box on the wall. Her hands were shaking and she typed in the incorrect code twice.

Now desperate to be out in the open, she scrabbled at the door. It slammed behind her with a bang. She had forgotten to switch off all the lights but she wasn't going back in. Knowing that her fear was out of proportion, she ran across the car park and pressed at the key fob again and again. The damn thing wasn't working. She remembered dropping her keys in a puddle earlier. The water must have got in. Her heart was hammering in her throat. She flicked the metal of the backup key from the plastic and fumbled in the darkness to find the car's lock. She was sure that come morning, she would find a thousand scratches and scuffs to the paintwork as she had repeatedly tried to insert the key. When she finally managed to open it, the sound of the car door unlocking was almost too much. Blood suddenly rushed to her face, making her head throb and in one quick movement, she snatched at the door, opened it and got in.

Turning instinctively, she locked the driver's door and then, still feeling unsafe, she dived across the central column, jarring her ribs on the gear stick, so that she might ensure the passenger door was secure also.

Only then did she exhale. She hadn't realised that she had been holding her breath, and she felt a giddy, head rush as she sat with her hands on the steering wheel.

'Oh God, what an idiot,' she said to herself. Her lips were tingling and she tried to relax her shoulders. 'You're fine,' she said angrily.

As she drove the ten minutes, she kept her eyes firmly on the road, not wanting to look this way or that, for fear of losing concentration. *Just get home. Not much further.* She glanced in the rear mirror several times, seeing headlights behind her. *They're not following. They're going home, just like you.* Cathy signalled to turn up her road. She looked in the mirror once more. Was the car behind her going to signal also? No. She sighed in relief. They hadn't signalled. She was nearly home and she was fine. Home, food, bed.

She slowed and turned left, following the road up towards her house. Again, she glanced in the mirror. Although the car hadn't signalled, the headlights were still behind her. Panic began to spread through her once more and her heart began to thump faster.

'Damn it,' she whispered. 'Leave me alone, for God's sake.'

What should she do? It was foolish to stop the car. If she did that, she was a sitting duck. Should she turn the car and instead drive directly to the police station? This person was stalking her. The car had slowed and was right behind her now, refusing to pass even though she had pulled in. Cathy allowed her car to crawl along, still hoping that she had made a mistake. She was so close to home. In an impulsive gesture, she slammed on her brakes, put on her hazard warning lights and sounded her horn again and again.

The car behind her rapidly signalled and passed her, accelerating away. She was too distressed to look for a faulty tail light that she knew must be there. She sat until a concerned neighbour came out of their house and crossed the street. The man tapped on the window and Cathy wasn't sure how long it took her to unclench her fists from the steering wheel. She looked up at the figure by the car, her eyes confused and unseeing.

'Oh, see? I said I thought it was you, Dr Moreland, and usually it's us making a racket. What happened?' This was all relayed through the closed window. Cathy stared at the man, not recognising him. Then, something in her mind seemed to click and she shook her head trying to clear it.

'Sorry. I accidentally pressed the horn.'

The man didn't hear right. He tapped on the window again. 'What? Wind down your window, I can't hear. Need to come in and see you about my ears.' He laughed.

Cathy didn't smile. She nodded and releasing the handbrake drove the final twenty yards to her own house. She was aware that her neighbour was crossing the street to continue the conversation but ignoring him, she stumbled up the drive and finally unlocking it, collapsed against her closed door.

17

'Knock, knock,' Cathy said, poking her head around James's door. 'Peace offering.' She produced a mug of tea and placed it on the desk in front of him.

James sighed and leaned back in his chair.

'Before you say anything,' she said, 'I know you're right. There has been a lot going on and I've been taking on too much. I'm always snappy when I'm pressured and it's always the people who mean the most to me that get the worst of it.' She smiled. 'Sorry that was you. You're very important to me.'

He picked up his mug and took a sip. 'After all these years and still, you make a rubbish cup of tea.' His face was deadly serious, and her heart sank. But then, his features relaxed and he smiled. 'Oh, sit down, for goodness' sake. You're a pig-headed so-and-so at times.'

'I couldn't sleep last night,' she confessed. 'I kept going over and over what I said to you.'

He shrugged. 'I've forgotten, but I'm sure you must know I'm not being deliberately interfering.'

She nodded. 'I'll see Stuart,' she said. 'I've already decided. He told me to book in anyway. I'm overdue an MOT.'

'Go later today. Linda's in and there are free appointments so we can do without you for an hour.'

She drove to the Westfield Practice after her morning surgery. Stuart Kidd had done just as he promised and fitted her in without question. He was very accommodating like that.

She had to drive along the Ancrum Road to head out of town. She felt that she knew the stretch far too well after all of her toing and froing that week. But rather than slowing as she came to the gates to Balmuir House, she instead accelerated past, wanting to put as great a distance from herself and the place as possible. She thought of dreadful Archie, rattling around the place, full of bitterness about his brother and not caring if he ever saw the man again, it seemed. What had Adam done to deserve such treatment? There had been a long-standing family rift. She recalled again Archie's words. He had mentioned their other brother, Eddie. Cathy wondered if this had indeed been the dark obnoxious man who had passed her in his car on the first night she had come to look for Mr Steer. Had he too been the man who had come to her practice to tamper with the computers? The description certainly seemed to fit.

The road snaked onwards. The fields spanned out in front of her, mostly harvested now and some still with a sprinkling of frost from the overnight lows. Westfield was six miles west of Glainkirk and the drive took a little over five minutes from the outskirts.

Dr Kidd took her in almost straight away, closing the door behind whilst indicating she should sit.

'And your sleep pattern? How has that been? The last time you were in, you mentioned an issue after a busy day's work.' He leaned back in the chair and spoke conversationally as if he was a concerned friend rather than a clinician.

Cathy smiled weakly and then deciding to be quite frank. Her words came in an untidy rush. 'Not so good, Stuart. Not really, these past few weeks.' She stopped abruptly. Her hands had been tightly clenched in her lap and she unclasped them having finally spoken, feeling her knuckles click and pop in protest.

'Eating?' he asked.

Cathy grimaced, knowing full-well that she could hardly tell him she was. She waited.

The other doctor uncrossed his legs.

'It's always been an issue for you. I'm just thinking of warning signs. Have you noticed your mood changing at all, Cathy? I can see things have been a strain recently. Is it due to anything in particular? Last time you were here, you and...' He leaned forward and touched the mouse beside his computer. He scrolled up through her notes. She could have helped him, but instead, sat in silence, watching as if from afar. 'He was in your year at med school. A surgical registrar? It was Chris, wasn't it?'

'It was. It isn't now.'

'Oh. I'm sorry. The last time you were in, he had moved into your place. You were happy. You said things were quite serious.'

'They were.'

No one else had known. She certainly hadn't confided in her own GP. It had been so early on, and they had only enjoyed the secret for a matter of three weeks before it had ended. She had miscarried at work, sitting alone in the staff toilets at the end of the doctors' corridor. She had been in the middle of her morning surgery. After she had cleaned herself up, she had headed back to her consulting room. She had carried on with her day as normal and waited until she was home to tell him. No point in making a fuss. Chris had been less upset than her. They had only been serious for six months and it had all happened too fast. Logic told her that it was for the best. In the end, the lie she told herself had driven a wedge between them.

There was a long pause. Dr Kidd's eyes were full of concern as he watched her. She felt rage and self-pity in equal measure and looked away. She knew that she wasn't making his job particularly easy. She made a dreadful patient at the best of times but talking about her private life so matter-of-factly was excruciating.

'Cathy...' he began.

'I know, I know,' she breathed, sweeping a strand of hair off her cheek. 'You're just doing your job. You were very decent to fit me in so promptly. If it were you, I'd do the same. I'd ask the same things and be infinitely sympathetic with your responses.' As she spat the last words out, the bitterness made her throat ache.

'If you'd rather see another doctor, I can arrange it. I know it's hard being on the other side.' He sighed. 'Listen, I've been there myself. At least I'm not examining you. Last year I had to go into A&E, remember I told you? I still cringe thinking about the bloody junior house officer blushing as she examined me.'

Cathy smiled. 'No, I know all that and please don't think I'm ungrateful. It's just...'

'It's just, you hate it being this way. But it is, Cathy. We do this every few months. It's the first opportunity to pick up a problem. I'm as determined to keep you at work as you are. You know that. I'll do everything I can to keep you healthy. Honestly, do you think things are slipping again?'

Cathy looked to the ceiling. 'A bit,' she admitted. Her eyes flicked up at him, and then away. 'Chris and I finished a month or so back. Not long after I was in. That hasn't helped. I've probably taken on more at the practice to keep me occupied. We're pretty busy at the moment, I don't know about you?'

He nodded, perhaps relieved that the conversation had moved on to safer ground. 'As always,' he admitted in shared understanding. 'You've lost weight though, clearly,' he said.

'I know.'

'Sleep?'

'Not great.'

'Racing thoughts? Overvalued ideas? Paranoia?'

Cathy knew he meant well, and in truth, she would rather have the symptoms of her hypomania reeled off quickly. It didn't do to dwell too long on them.

'Overthinking perhaps,' she conceded, 'but nothing too out-of-the-way. I wouldn't say paranoia, but jumpy, for sure.'

'Any thoughts of self-harm, suicidal ideation?'

'No. None this time.'

'Good. Obviously, good.' He laughed. 'Okay, what are you thinking about with the medication? I assume you're taking it regularly still?'

Cathy nodded. She had learnt from previous mistakes that going without her antipsychotic tablets would send her into a bipolar crisis within a very short time. When she had initially presented some three or four years ago, she had stubbornly attempted to self-medicate, in part with alcohol. The wine, or vodka, or whatever she happened to have in, helped to dull her competing thoughts but it had done nothing for her mood. For that, she had taken mild opiates from the stores at work. They had helped for a short while, but she had quickly become emotionally dependent on them. It was very much in the past, but now, every time she returned to either a psychiatrist or her own GP for a review, she knew that they would know. It would be on her medical records for life.

'I could speak to psychiatry and consider upping your dose,' Dr Kidd cut in. 'Or,' he said, thinking aloud, 'we could always consider adding in a short-term anxiolytic possibly? Had you had any thoughts about it yourself?'

Cathy shook her head.

'Listen,' he said, leaning forward in his chair. 'I am concerned. I've been worried since I saw you at the gym. I don't want to make more out of it than needs be, but the vasovagal? I assume that was a one-off, Cathy?'

Cathy sat rigid in her seat.

'Listen, really, these things happen from time to time. Do you mind today if we check your bloods while you're here? It makes sense to run a set of general tests to be sure you're not anaemic to top it all. It's more for my peace of mind than anything.'

'There's no need. James did a test already.'

He raised his eyebrows. 'So, you had been worried yourself?' He paused. 'Better to have the bloods done here. You know that. Then they go on your record. Otherwise, if something happened–'

'Oh, we all need to cover our backs,' Cathy suddenly said spitefully.

'I didn't mean...'

'Of course, you didn't, but what a weight of responsibility it must be to have me on your books. If something goes wrong and I accidentally kill a patient, the first place they'd come looking is here. The buck would stop with you. You've been doing the assessments and clearing me fit to work after all.' Cathy shook her head in disgust.

'Cathy...'

'Don't bother. We're not colleagues, or friends when I'm sitting in this chair. You have to do your job. Go on then.' She got up and clumsily pulled off her jacket and rolled up her sleeve. 'Do it. Hurry up and take the blood sample. Do it now.' She glared at him, challenging him to refuse.

He got up, but rather than wrapping a tourniquet around her arm, he gently rolled her sleeve back down.

'Cathy, sit down, please. You know I'd never force you to do anything you didn't want. I can see things have been a strain. What was it you were saying about finding James's replacement when we spoke last? Have you got any further?'

Feeling suddenly ashamed, Cathy flushed. 'We don't even have our other partner at work at the moment. Had to go back to Ireland for a family crisis, so I've not had a chance to talk to him about our options. Like you said though, we'll not find anyone in a hurry.'

'Perhaps I was being a little pessimistic. I'll keep an ear out.'

There was a pause.

'How are we leaving things? If I'm completely honest, I feel that you're going downhill again and if I didn't know the full background, I'd be suggesting you take a bit of time off work to recharge at the very least. I'd say a psychiatric assessment again wouldn't go amiss. Even if it's just to adjust your medication.' He looked at her and smiled. 'I can see you're not happy with that. You tell me what we should do.'

Cathy sighed. 'I haven't a clue, Stuart,' she confessed. 'As for dropping hours, you know I can't. I'm even signed up to do an out-of-hours shift this evening.'

He glanced out of the window as someone passed and looked in. 'Sorry,' he said, reaching up and drawing the blinds. 'They shouldn't cross through. We've put up enough signs. It's a staff car park, but it seems they're all trying to squeeze in when the other's full.'

'I did,' Cathy admitted. 'I thought it'd be okay.'

'Oh, you're all right,' he said. 'I only got irate when some old boy reversed into the back of my car a few weeks back. That's why I'm twitchy.'

Something inside Cathy went cold. 'You're still driving an Audi?'

'Yes,' he said. 'Good car. Sorry, Cathy, back to you. What will we do then?'

But Cathy's attitude had changed. 'Thinking about it, I agree with what you've said. I'd better see psychiatry,' she admitted.

He looked surprised. 'If you're sure...'

'If you'd do a referral for me, that would be super, Stuart. Sorry to have made such a fuss. You're right. The pressure does get on top of me at times.'

'We'll not adjust the tablets until you see a consultant then?'

'Good plan. Thanks, and as I say, I'm sorry, really I am.' Getting up, she smiled. 'Thanks again. You are a dear friend and I know I can be ungrateful at times.'

As she left, she hoped she'd not been too abrupt in her change of mind. She returned to her car, glancing as she did so at the black Audi parked at the far end of the car park with the rear light smashed.

18

Cathy was at a loss. Who could she trust now? The rear light smashed on Dr Kidd's car could only really mean one thing. He had been trailing her. When she thought about it, it made sense, and yet it confused her so greatly. Why would he of all people want to follow her? Had it been his car she had seen outside the Steer's house the night she had gone to look for Mr Steer? Was Dr Kidd in some way involved in the couple's disappearance? It seemed too bizarre to imagine. Cathy thought back to what she knew about the night Mrs Steer had disappeared. Of course, Dr Kidd had been on duty for the out-of-hours service. He had been ready to take over just as Euan had finished his shift. She had assumed that he had stayed at the base, but she may have been wrong. She hadn't thought to ask. As soon as she had found out that Euan had done a late call alone off the Ancrum Road, she had thought it could only be him. Cathy thought back guiltily to how she had jumped to the conclusion. She had thought Euan had been the one to visit the Steers. Due to his absence, of course, she'd not been able to speak to him about it. Even that had seemed wrong, but supposing Dr Kidd had been the one to go out to the house that night to answer Mr Steer's concerned call about his wife? Was Cathy to believe in full all that Mr Steer had told her?

In her consulting room with the door closed, she considered the problem. 'Why won't anything make any sense?' she asked herself.

At the sink she washed her hands, running the water until it was so hot it nearly burned her and her hands turned red and raw. She pumped the pink hand sanitiser and allowed the gel to pool in her cupped palms. Then she lathered it, doing as she had done a thousand times before. Why couldn't she make any headway? She could almost understand there being some family secret that the Steer family wanted to bury, but why involve a local family doctor in the whole thing?

Cathy had known Dr Kidd for many years. Granted, they had never socialised, but she had met him frequently professionally and then recently, he had taken her on as a patient too. Of all people, she couldn't understand why he would be involved with the Steers. And was she to believe that he had been the doctor who had gone out to see Mrs Steer that night? Was he meant to have locked Mrs Steer's husband in his spare room and then spirited her away?

Cathy thought back to what Mr Steer had told her about the night. Dr Kidd would be highly unlikely to suggest the diagnosis of meningitis and then wrongly recommend a cold bath. But then again, she had been almost ready to believe Euan might. She supposed that she had known Euan for less time, despite working alongside him. He had qualified more recently too, of course. If only he had been around to answer her questions now.

She crossed her room and pulled a fresh paper sheet over the examination couch, ready for the next patient. The one thing she did know was that Dr Kidd's car had been following her. She thought back to the night at the gym when she was sure she was being followed. She had looked in the rear mirror and seen the faulty light of the car. What were the chances of there being more than one car in the car park with a broken left rear light? No, it could only have been Dr Kidd. He had taken an unusual interest in the Steers. Perhaps he knew the family or had some vested interest in the situation.

Was it something to do with the business? Cathy knew nothing really about the firm Traxium. She did recall Linda mentioning her husband's involvement in the distribution of influenza vaccines in the UK. Was Dr Kidd in some way tangled in the business also? If he was short of cash. Was it possible that he was working privately for Traxium? There was no legal reason why he should not. Why then had he been following her though, unless he had become twitchy about her interest in the family? Was Traxium a less altruistic company than anyone had supposed?

Cathy thought about Dr Kidd that morning and his charming, easy manner. She thought of the concern he had shown her over the years since her mental health had come into question. Now, she began to doubt the genuineness of even that. He had been so adamant today that she should change her tablets and see psychiatry. Cathy shook her head. How stupid she had been, but if she couldn't trust her GP, who could she trust? The most important thing that morning had been to get out of his consulting room. Cathy still couldn't believe that the man would have done her any harm. It seemed so out of character, but she had known that she needed to get out. Perhaps Dr Kidd might not have meant to hurt her, but it appeared that he had somehow fallen into some murky business and with two people vanished, Cathy had no intention of endangering herself.

Bending over her desk, she checked the computer. Five minutes until her first one was due in. She straightened up and cast her mind back to the night at the gym when she had fainted. She suddenly recalled Dr Kidd's suggestion to give her a quick injection of something to help her pulse rate come up. What had he been planning to inject her with? It was hardly protocol for a simple vasovagal. And then, what of the blood tests he had wanted to perform just that day? Cathy shook her head. She couldn't go on like this, though. She would drive herself half-mad.

Before starting her afternoon surgery, she should at least get a hot drink. She had skipped lunch yet again and her stomach groaned. In the staff room, she hurriedly dropped a teabag in a mug and poured in the hot water. She was just squeezing the bag with the back of her spoon when the door opened.

'Oh God! You made me start. I didn't know anyone was up here,' Linda said, coming in.

Cathy crossed the small kitchen and dropped her used teabag in the bin. 'Only me. Kettle's just this second boiled.'

'Thanks,' Linda said, taking the offered mug. 'How's it been anyway? Haven't seen you all day, or yesterday, when I think of it.'

'Fine,' Cathy said, although, by her pale face and hunched shoulders, it must have been obvious to Linda that she was feeling the strain.

'That good?' Linda laughed. 'I was hoping to have a quiet word with you as it happens, but I've just not managed to catch you. Nothing urgent but I had heard rumours about James and I thought I should at least put some feelers out. Had you and Euan thought about how you plan to replace him yet?'

In truth, Cathy could have done without the conversation, but knowing that it must have taken some guts to ask, she smiled at Linda. 'I need to talk to Euan when he returns. We'll be advertising of course. Are you interested, Linda? I thought with the kids being the age they are, you were reluctant to commit.'

Linda grimaced. 'Complicated,' she said. 'Pete's having his hours cut, so I might need to step up.'

'Oh?' Cathy asked. Did this mean that Traxium were indeed in financial difficulty? 'We'll be looking for an eight or nine session partner to replace James,' she said. 'Think about it, Linda. It's a huge commitment. I myself only do seven and it's full-on. I'm sorry to hear about Pete, though. Any reason why his hours are being dropped?'

Cathy was sure that there was a flash of annoyance in Linda's expression, but if there had been, the salaried GP covered it up fast.

'Just the financial climate, I suppose,' she said vaguely. 'I'll speak to him about me taking on more sessions tonight.'

Cathy felt rather sick as she descended the stairs to begin consulting. She knew that Linda would be a dreadful choice of partner, and she hoped that she would see sense and not apply for the position. Linda had shown little interest in the business side of the practice since she had arrived. She had waived the suggestion to take on some of the trainees and had refused any out-of-hours shifts also.

Cathy called in her first patient of the afternoon. It was going to be a long day. She was working that evening also, covering out-of-hours and she hoped the shift wouldn't prove too hectic after a full day's work at the practice. Cathy thought of her own little house, of its empty cupboards and cold floors. A place that should be a sanctuary, no longer felt like one. Tonight, of all nights she was glad not to head straight home. In many ways, she felt safer at work.

19

The afternoon was bright and clear but the evening temperature had already dropped below zero. Cathy tugged the edges of her jacket and ran the zip up to her neck. She had spoken briefly with James before leaving and he told her that they might expect Euan back the following day. This was a relief in many ways. The workload had not been unmanageable without him, but the other doctors had been stretched, without a doubt. Michelle had tried to acquire a locum to help but it seemed that everyone was booked up. Cathy mentioned Linda's query about the partnership to James. Of course, he wouldn't have a formal say in who replaced him, but having more experience than most in the hiring and firing of staff over the years, it seemed quite natural to ask.

'It's tricky.' He sighed. 'Linda's been a godsend this last year or so. She's been loyal to the practice too.'

Cathy frowned, feeling guilty for even voicing the concern. 'I'm not doubting her ability or commitment, it's more the extra responsibility. The hours worry me too. She's left early again this evening. Michelle said it was a problem with the nursery. It's not had an impact on us yet, but as a partner... Well, just think of all the extra things we do outwith work hours.'

James nodded. 'Well, there lies your answer then. I assume you wanted to replace like with like? Eight or nine sessions wouldn't suit Linda anyway if she can hardly stay for the ones she's doing now as a salaried doctor.'

'I feel awkward. I don't want to offend her. You know that in theory, we could take her on as a partner and just advertise for more hours in a salaried doctor instead, to cover her shortfall.'

'Don't make any rash decisions,' James advised. 'If it's simply a case of not wanting to rock the boat and offend someone, then I think it's a very poor reason to offer a partnership. You don't want to regret your decision a year or two down the line. And remember, you'll be the senior partner if you take on Linda. She has no interest in the business side of things so you'll have no help on that front. I know Euan's been excellent, but he too has little experience with anything other than the clinical work.'

At the time, Cathy had sighed and told James that it all still required a good deal of thought. She needed to have a long chat with Euan to see how he felt about things. But quite apart from the pressures at work, Cathy wanted to see Euan to clear the air over the out-of-hours situation. If it was indeed the case that he had done a late call alone, he had endangered himself and made a rash error of judgement. He had been wanting to do the right thing, by all accounts in saving his driver and Dr Kidd the hassle of the late visit, but it did show a lack of foresight that worried her.

She found herself casting her mind back to when she had first become a partner. James had been hugely supportive of her and as she had tentatively settled herself into her role, he had been there to guide her. She should offer Euan the same. Cathy thought of her now-late partner. Mark had been the main force driving the practice forwards for a good number of years. In dealing with people, he had been brash at times but his dedication to the practice was never in question. Losing him had been both a tragedy and the end of an era for the place. When he died, the impetus seemed to dissipate from all of the team. They had drifted since. Euan had been a success, but he had not stepped up to the mark yet. It would be hard now to replace James too, if not impossible. Perhaps then, they shouldn't try and substitute like with like. Maybe the entire practice needed a change of vision. Cathy wondered if she was the one to do it. Her own health had come into question and without a strong team around her, she doubted she would have the strength to pull things together.

Having left the practice, she parked outside the out-of-hours base. She had bought a sandwich from the little corner shop on the way there and that would do as her evening meal. Her key fob had dried out and was working once again. She locked the car and crossed the glistening tarmac to the building. Outside in the bracing air, the remnants of the day were receding. Her breath was a cloud of white. She glanced to the right and saw the out-of-hours cars parked in their usual spots near the door. The drivers took great pride in their vehicles. The hub had two cars currently in service. Both had reflective stickers along the sides and a green light on top in case they had to dash out to a genuine emergency. Thankfully these things were relatively rare. Since she had begun working for the out-of-hours team, Cathy had only asked her driver to green light her a handful of times. She thought that the drivers quite enjoyed the adrenaline rush of an emergency. It probably broke up an otherwise dull occupation and added to their self-image knowing that they might run a red light in the town, leaving other motorists to pull into the side as they approached.

Dave was by the door when she arrived.

'Evening,' she said. 'I didn't think we were on together tonight. All okay?'

Dave nodded. 'Just nipping out to get something from the car. Yes, you've got me again, I'm afraid. I'm doing evening and an all-nighter.' He chuckled. 'Poor Reg called in sick at the last minute. Got some tummy bug. I didn't mind,' he reassured her. 'Wife's still in. Leg not improved at all. They've tried her with three antibiotics now, and nothing's making a difference.'

'You should be with her,' Cathy said.

Dave shrugged. 'That's ten days she's been in. Nightmare for us. No, I'm better earning what I can here. I was in seeing her earlier anyway.'

Cathy smiled and touched his arm.

He nodded but didn't speak.

'Have you been inside yet? How's it looking so far?'

'No visits yet and I think you've only two phone-backs to do. Neither sounded like they'd need urgent attention.'

'Listen, nip out and get something to eat if you haven't brought it with you. I grabbed a sandwich on the way here. Then, if it gets busy later, you'll not be needing to get something. Are you doing from now until this morning straight?'

Dave nodded. 'It's Dr Kidd on with me again later after you. We're getting well acquainted these past few months, the two of us.'

'Stuart on again? He must be mad,' she said.

'Maybe work's more fun than home for him. At least I don't need to worry on that front.'

Cathy smiled. 'She'll be home soon, I hope.'

'Right. She'd usually send me in with something to eat that she'd made specially. I've been living on takeaways for the past week. I'll nip out now then if you'll not miss me. I'll only be fifteen minutes. Better take my car rather than the out-of-hours one, though. Don't want to stink that one up with greasy food. Can I get you anything? Poke of chips even?'

Cathy shook her head.

'No stealing from mine then,' Dave warned her and chuckled.

Cathy headed inside, stamping her feet on the mat by the door before going through. The base had been purpose-built several years ago alongside the community centre in town and was easily accessed by the locals. Cathy walked through the small waiting area, passing the three consulting rooms. They rarely had more than one doctor working, and currently, one of the rooms was being used as a bit of a makeshift store for some of the medical equipment and supplies. The end room was generally used by the night-shift doctor. Although it was a functioning consulting room with an examination couch and all the paraphernalia required for seeing patients, it was also at the back of the base and if things were quiet overnight, it was a good spot to catch a couple of hours sleep. Cathy assumed that this was what Dr Kidd had been doing these past few months. It seemed impossible for the man to function the following day at work after a full night shift.

Cathy moved through to the staff room beyond the waiting area. Here, the doctors and drivers often sat together during a shift. She had brought in a packet of biscuits and a small bottle of milk to contribute to the overnight staff's supplies. She laid these by the kettle and crossed the room to the computer, removing her jacket and draping it over the back of a large armchair. This was where the overnight driver might sleep. In front of the recliner chair was a large television. The doctors had clubbed together last Christmas and bought it as a thank you to the drivers for all of their hard work. Before that, they had listened to the radio, but the television had been a big hit. If a shift was relatively peaceful, the little staff room could be a very pleasant place to settle.

She saw Dave's jacket on the chair and crossed to look at a book he'd brought in. Picking it up, she turned the hardback over; a library copy of a grim-looking Stephen King. Cathy wasn't a fan of horror stories especially when they were centred around lethal pandemics. Real life was quite complicated enough as it was. She put the book down and shook her head. She couldn't remember the last time she'd had a chance to read a book. At the other side of the TV was a stack of medical journals. That was where her attention was more often taken.

Cathy seated herself at the computer and logged in so that the service might recognise she had begun her shift. She scrolled through the list of patient contacts so far. Dave was right. It wouldn't take her long to deal with the two who had requested a callback. One, she knew already so it would make things even easier. She quickly called both, advising the first over the telephone and asking the other to come down to the base in the next half hour so that she might examine them. With this dealt with, and still alone, she quickly checked through the out-of-hours doctors' bag, as she always did when she started her shift. It was a requirement of all of the GPs to keep track of the bag's contents and replace any items used, but having arrived at a visit only last month to find that she had no intravenous frusemide, Cathy had become even more particular. Today it seemed that all the drugs were up to date and in their correct slots, though. She checked the large compartment in the bag for medical equipment and tutted, seeing that both a stethoscope and pen torch had not been put back. Cathy spent a good five minutes hunting, but giving up, she jogged along the corridor to one of the treatment rooms and put an old stethoscope and torch in the bag instead. She would leave a note on the board for whoever had pocketed the equipment accidentally, to replace them as soon as they realised. With this taken care of, she settled herself at the computer and she scrolled back to the night that Mr Steer said he had called the out-of-hours team. To be honest, after checking his medical records on the practice computer and finding them missing, she hardly expected to see anything. Whoever had got rid of the person, had been intelligent enough to erase all record of them also.

Cathy leaned in and read the night's entries. It had been a steady night for Euan it seemed, but come eleven o'clock when Dr Kidd had taken over there had been only a couple of callbacks, neither of which had required a visit. As she had anticipated, Marjorie Steer was not on the computer. Cathy rested back in her chair. It was fine. She'd have almost been disappointed to find that they'd slipped up in missing that detail from their clear-up operation. She thought back to the effort whoever it was had gone to. It had been excessive, to say the least. The Steer family though, if they had wanted to, would have access to every possible resource to make someone disappear. She was just taking one last look at the screen when there was a sound from behind.

She barely had a chance to turn before he spoke and to him, it probably couldn't have looked worse.

20

'Well, Cathy,' he said. He spoke with a conversational tone, but she knew only too well that his mind must surely be racing. 'Fancy seeing you here.'

She laughed and tried to make herself a barrier between him and the screen. 'Oh, I heard you were coming back tomorrow. Good to see you, Euan,' she said, but her voice shook and her mouth was now dry. 'I'm sorry to hear about your grandmother, really I am. Did the funeral go okay? We've been thinking of you.'

'As well as could be expected,' he shrugged. She saw him glancing over her shoulder and knew that he must be able to see the screen. Desperately she tried to think of a reason for looking at his patient list for the last night he was on-call, but he was talking already and she couldn't think.

'So, you're on-call this evening, are you? I hadn't realised. I came in as I was passing by. I left behind a book that I was reading the other night. Thought I'd pop back and collect it. Didn't have much of a chance to read during that last shift I was on. Too busy. Although, you've seen that for yourself.'

Cathy swallowed. Her heart was beating fast and she had

gone suddenly very cold. 'Oh, not as such,' she said, trying to sound casual. 'Stuart Kidd and I had been discussing a patient when I last bumped into him and I was trying to see when they'd been seen. He thought it was during an overnight shift here.'

'What was the name?' His eyes were chilling and did not move from her own. He didn't believe a word she had just said.

She sighed in resignation. 'As it happens, I was looking at a late call that came in that night you were on. I did want a word about that last shift of yours. I'd heard you did the last call alone without a driver.'

Euan laughed bitterly and then crossed to the armchair and threw himself down. Cathy had never seen him behave in such a way and she wondered how well she knew the man she had worked alongside this last year. Gone was the jovial Irish banter, and in its place was a morose sulkiness. 'Am I getting my knuckles rapped?' he asked.

Cathy grimaced but didn't answer.

'It was a pleuritic chest pain, Cathy,' he said. 'Not some drug fiend requesting a visit. I was safe and there was no unnecessary risk taken, although I'm touched by your interest. You are pulling the senior partner card fast and James isn't even retired.'

Cathy turned in her chair. 'It's not that at all. Look, I don't want to make too much of this but there's a protocol for out-of-hours for a reason. Yes, you could endanger yourself going out alone, but carrying the medication is a risk to others also. If the drugs from the emergency bag had somehow fallen into the wrong hands...'

'How would they, Cathy?' he asked wearily. 'I was doing Stuart Kidd a favour. He's been taking far too many overnights and I could see that the last thing he wanted to do was to have to run out along the Ancrum Road to a chest pain as soon as he started his shift. And there was the driver too. From what I heard; he's been having problems at home as well. I was being nice. It's what we're meant to do as part of a team. We take the strain when others are feeling it.'

'We're all feeling it,' she answered, still a little shakily. She'd never called him out over a decision before. Perhaps that was the problem.

'Well, some are feeling the strain more than others, clearly,' he said.

There was a long pause. She couldn't quite believe how he had spoken to her.

They stared at one another for some moments and then he sighed heavily. 'Listen, a close relative of mine has just died. I've only just got home. I thought I'd get a little more support from you of all people. You make me wonder if I did the right thing in the first place.'

She looked at him quizzically.

'Forget it. I'd better go.'

'What about your book?' But he was already at the door.

'Forget it,' he repeated.

'Euan, wait,' she called.

He paused with his hand on the door and she thought he was going to ignore her, but slowly he turned and shook his head. 'Sorry,' he said, and for the first time since he had come in, she saw a flicker of regret.

'Me too. I shouldn't have jumped on you as soon as you came in. There's a time and a place. We've missed having you around, Euan. Honestly, we have. Thankfully it's not been too busy but we were worried about you. You could've phoned me or James direct, you know? Like you say, we're meant to be supporting one another. I hope you didn't think we'd refuse if you asked for a leave of absence?'

'I'll be honest with you, Cathy. I wasn't thinking at all. I just knew I needed to get on a plane and get home. It was maybe stupid, but I didn't think. Look, all this stuff about the late visit. It's not such a big deal, is it? I mean, why are you so upset about the thing? It was a one-off. I don't usually do late calls alone.'

Cathy sighed. 'No. I think I got carried away. I've had a lot on my mind too. I told you before you left about the troubling patient I had in? Mr Steer, do you remember?'

He smiled. 'Surely, you've got to the bottom of that by now?'

'That's just it. I've not and I can't understand what happened that night. You see, I've not even told James this, but the records have disappeared. Vanished off our computer database. And I was looking on the out-of-hours computer too, just when you came in. There's no record of a visit request to Marjorie Steer the night Stuart took over from you.'

'But I could've told you that. Mr Steer didn't phone and ask for a call. I would've remembered. I think the issue has been with the story he told you in the first place. What's he saying about it now then? Have you seen him since? Is his wife still missing or has she miraculously turned up?'

Cathy snorted. 'They've both gone, along with all of their belongings. I went out to their house to see and the place has been gutted. I've been going around and around in circles trying to make sense of the thing. I get an uneasy feeling, you know?'

'So, what do you know about them? Hadn't they returned from India recently? Surely they've gone back. Do we know about relatives?'

'Well, that's a whole other issue. Mr and Mrs Steer were living at the lodge house of a mansion on the Ancrum Road. I thought that someone up at the mansion might be able to help so I knocked on their door.'

'Are they patients of ours then too?'

'Oh God no, they'll not be NHS. Very upmarket and the owner of the house seemed quite mad. It turns out that Mr Steer is his brother. He seemed to have a low opinion of both him and

Marjorie, his wife. Told me to butt out and that he was glad to see the back of them.'

'Why were they living in a lodge house then, and him up in a mansion if they were brothers?'

'That, I still don't know. There's obviously been some massive family feud.'

'I see. So, are you now thinking that the family have somehow disposed of Mr and Mrs Steer? It does sound a bit far-fetched, Cathy.'

She sighed. 'I know, I know. I don't know why the thing's bothered me so much. I've got enough to worry about.'

Euan raised his eyebrows as if in exaggerated agreement at this sentiment. 'These people aren't even on our list, you say now? Well, Cathy, surely, it's time to let the thing drop. We've got enough needy people already, who are deserving of your care, without identifying more.'

Cathy sighed.

'Have you spoken to anyone else about it?' Euan asked.

'Not really.' She sighed. 'I went to the gym to try and find out more about Mrs Steer. She was having an affair according to Linda but I didn't even manage to find out who the man was, although I have my suspicions. I've made a bit of a mess of things. I started to think someone didn't want me to know what had happened to them. I even got it into my head that I was being followed.'

'Leave it alone,' Euan urged. 'Honestly, it's not worth the bother, Cathy. These people sound horrible and the concern for them isn't justified. Listen, I'd better get home. Can we chat tomorrow, if you've got the time? I'll be in first thing.'

'Sure. I wanted to talk with you about James's retirement anyway. Linda approached me but I'm not sure... We'll have a good catch-up in the morning though.'

He turned at the door.

'Sorry about everything, you know?'

He smiled and left her. It was only when she was alone again and while she waited for Dave to return, that she wondered how tactful she had just been. When it came to the Steer family, how shrewd was it to confide in anyone?

21

'The footprint,' she said to herself when she woke the next morning.

She lay there for a moment, staring at the shadows on the ceiling. There was no light other than from her digital alarm, and this cast a greenish glow across her sheets. What did that even mean, the footprint? Confused she shook her head and then relaxed back against the pillows. Her hair felt damp and she raised her hand. Her forehead was roasting and the touch of her cold hand on it made her shiver. She dragged the duvet up and around her, huddling beneath the thick folds and wishing that the clock didn't say three. What about the footprint? Was it something from a dream? More likely a nightmare. She'd had plenty of those recently. She screwed up her eyes. No, there hadn't been a nightmare.

She had always been a poor sleeper, even back at university when she had established a routine of sleepwalking around the time of exams. It had caused much hilarity amongst her housemates. Once she had woken fully dressed in the shower having dreamt that she was late for the school bus. She thought it had only become worse since she was diagnosed with bipolar disorder. Sometimes she spoke in her sleep so loudly that she woke herself up and at other times, Chris had told her in the morning that he had been forced to lie partially on top of her to stop her from flailing about. She had told him it was probably due to the medication, but she had been on the tablets for so long that it was unlikely and the periods of disturbed sleep did seem to have a pattern of coming when she was at a crossroads in her life.

She lay half-dozing in a fuzziness that brought her close to the edge of sleep, without allowing her to completely fall in. She walked the edge of the abyss, feeling her way and longing for the nothingness. And then her foot sank deep into the mud. It stuck like clay. The footprint.

She was wide awake now and with trembling realisation, she thought how stupid she had been. She grabbed her dressing gown and hastily wrapped it around herself. Why hadn't she looked at the time? And why hadn't she gone back? Of course, there had to be something more at the lodge house. Without question, the larger footprint that she had seen in the flower border had belonged to someone peeping in the window, just as she had done. Someone had been creeping around the side of the house. If they had left behind a footprint, they had not been as clever as she had thought.

All along, Cathy had felt that she had been up against it. The speed with which lines of possible inquiry had been shut down had shown that she was dealing with a sophisticated operation. This was not some simple kidnapping at all. It had been planned and executed seamlessly. All evidence had been painstakingly managed, even down to the medical records of Mr and Mrs Steer. To destroy these had required intelligence and associates. What then of the footprint? Why would such a clever operation leave behind a telling clue like that?

Cathy found herself downstairs in her kitchen. The wall

clock told her that it was now three thirty. She filled the kettle and as she waited for it to boil, she took a banana from the fruit bowl and absent-mindedly peeled it. It was overripe having been sat there for far too long but she bit into the creamy sweet fruit and savoured it. Yes. She'd have to return to the lodge house but how would she go about it? She could hardly walk up to the mansion and ask them if they'd lend her a spare key, not after the dreadful encounter with Archie Steer. No, that wouldn't work at all. The only thing for it was to break in. Cathy didn't much like the idea. She had once before climbed in someone's window unasked to guarantee a patient's safety. Cathy wondered if she'd have the guts to go through with it alone. But she had little choice if she was to get to the bottom of things.

The kettle had boiled and she made herself a mug of tea. The hot bitter liquid soon warmed her. She'd do it today. She would be amazed if the kidnappers had left anything behind but even if they'd cleaned the place from top to bottom, she still wanted to look again at that footprint. She might find others or even tyre tracks. Why had she left it so long in looking? She had gone about the whole business in quite the wrong way.

Cathy sat at the kitchen table, cradling her mug in her hands, no longer noticing the overnight chill of the house. The thing that concerned her of course, was being caught. She imagined Archie or the other dark man who had driven past that first night, presumably Eddie the other brother, catching her while she was trying to break in. She wondered how she might go unseen. She had walked around the back of the lodge house and she thought that if she could force a window, this would be by far the best place to do it, rather than within view of the road. But what about her car? And not only this, what about the person who had already been trailing her? Whether it was Dr Kidd or not, she knew that they didn't want her interfering in the business. How could she break in without alerting their attention too?

Driving to the lodge wasn't going to be a possibility, she decided. Her car felt like it had a flashing beacon on the roof. Cathy, for the first time, wondered if her car had been bugged with some kind of tracking device. It seemed that whenever she was in it, the driver with the faulty tail light seemed to know where she was.

She sipped at her tea again and thought about this disturbing new idea. But if she didn't drive, there was only one option. Balmuir house though was a good six miles by road. *You used to run ten miles for fun when you were at university*, her head told her. That was years ago though, and she wasn't fit, or as young anymore. *But you never lose your muscle memory*, the voice said. *Five, six miles is barely a warm-up. You could cut off a good mile and a half of that if you went off-road and ran along the field drills.*

Cathy placed her mug on the table and went to the cupboard under the stairs. She opened the door and was met by a blast of cold air. There was no insulation fitted and the wind from outside was blowing under the house and through the floorboards. Cathy flicked the light switch and a bare bulb on the sloping wall sprang into light, dazzling her for a second until her eyes grew accustomed to it. She knelt and began to rummage, knowing that they must be there. They were right at the back of course, under the ridiculous moon-boots she had bought on a whim and the wellingtons that she rarely needed. She held them up and looked thoughtfully. A bit scuffed but they would be fine. At least they'd not been chewed at by mice.

Cathy placed her running shoes on the radiator to warm through and returned to the kitchen. Her heart had begun to quicken at the prospect of what she was about to do. Did she have the courage to jog to Balmuir House and break into their lodge house? She thought for some minutes about what she might need to take with her. A head torch was a definite. She might also need some sort of tool to jam under a window frame. She went to the cupboard under the kitchen sink where she kept her little toolbox. It had a couple of screwdrivers, a hammer and a chisel. All had been given to her by her father when she had asked him from time to time for advice on fixing things. More often than not, he had ended up doing the little jobs himself, but he had left behind a few things in case she needed them. Of course, Chris had been quick to take on any jobs of that kind when he had been living there. She again found herself longing for his reassurance, knowing that he would have been beside her all the way if he had been around still. Putting this thought from her mind, she chose the chisel. It might be awkward to explain why she was carrying it if she met anyone while running but she already knew that she wouldn't be going in broad daylight and she'd have her rucksack.

Cathy had lain awake on enough occasions watching the glimmer of light begin to touch the edges of her curtains to know exactly when she might go. The sun would rise fully at six. Her hands were trembling now at the prospect but she knew that she must do it this morning before she changed her mind. She looked at the clock in her kitchen. It was now just after four. If she was going to leave her house at five when she judged she'd have the benefit of darkness on the roads but the first glimmer of light as she reached the trickier ground going through fields, she'd need to get ready.

She recalled the advice of her running coach at university from all those years ago. Never run on empty, he had told her. If she was going to have the stamina to do it, she'd need to fuel her body with more than a banana and not immediately before running or she might be sick. With freshened determination, Cathy set out her head torch and chisel. She would need water, she decided too. She placed all of the items beside a small rucksack. In this, she also put her purse, keys and phone just in case. She made herself a sandwich, which she ate as slowly as she dared and then climbed the stairs to dress.

It was five to five and her heart was in her throat when she opened her front door. She looked up the road to her neighbours' house and saw their porch light was still on. Otherwise, the night would have still been quite dark. Quietly, Cathy stepped out onto her drive and pulled the door behind her. *No going back*, she said to herself and with trepidation and thrill, she set out into the deep navy blue of the early morning, her feet finding comfort in the long-forgotten rhythm as they hit the tarmac.

22

For the first fifteen minutes, her body screamed. *Push through*, she told herself. *This won't last.* Gradually, with every deep draw through her nose, her lungs became more accustomed to the chill of the air. Then, her breathing settled. The white cloud of mist escaping with every exhalation, warmed her cheeks as she ran into it. It had always been the same. The first few minutes would be agonising even when she had been young and fit, although she hadn't recalled it feeling as bad as this. It was almost as if her body was going into panic mode and trying to force her to rethink her decision to run at all.

She tried to concentrate on parts of her body to distract herself. Her arms, her hands, the angle that her feet met the ground, doing anything, making the smallest of adjustments to make the effort seem less. Her fingers and her ears nipped with the cold, but soon she forgot to notice as she concentrated instead on the breath. She heard her coach's voice telling her to lean into the stride and to centre herself, allowing her arms to do the work. It was so long ago since she had last run like this and the pain of it made her almost giddy.

The first three miles were by streets that she knew well. She had already planned the quickest route in her head and she ran, hugging the edge of the road rather than the uneven pavements, and finding the straightest lines she could. There was no traffic initially and the isolation and stillness were exhilarating and she passed houses she had visited professionally, recalling the residents' faces. She imagined them now, stirring in bed perhaps as they heard the slap of her feet on the ground outside, then turning over they might drift off to sleep once more.

Her legs began to eat up the black tarmac, each step sending the road flicking past, slick and oily and wet. In places, a very thin frost had formed and as she rounded a corner at the end of St Andrew's Road, she slid, but flinging her arms out instinctively, rebalanced and continued, her heart hammering even harder in her aching chest. Her breath came in regular even heaves now that she had found her natural pace. She didn't run her fastest, just enough to keep the road moving under her feet. She turned right along Dalfair Street and then left onto the wider Park Grove. A cat scooted out from beneath a parked car, making her leap in fear. She swerved and then set her rhythm again finding a song in her head just to keep her moving.

She reached the end of Ninian Street, passing the sheltered housing complex there. Outside in the courtyard, a light shone and she glanced sideways and saw one of the wardens wafting away a telltale fog of grey-yellow smoke from her lips. Cathy raised her eyebrows but knew she'd not been seen. She crossed to a cycle track that would bring her level with the park. The rain over the preceding days had left the ground saturated and boggy. She ran on grass for a short distance, but the heaviness of the marshy land drained everything from her legs and she leapt back onto the path. Already, her legs were smattered with the grainy mud from the roads and after the first sharp intake of breath at the icy puddle water on her shins, she ploughed on, in many ways grateful for any distraction from the burning ache in her lungs.

The track by the park was bumpy and the puddles were only visible seconds before she was on them. Twice her ankle flicked and she caught herself just before she tripped. The second time, she stumbled and cried out in pain.

You could take a breather and give the ankle a minute, a voice in her head said, but she'd heard that coaxing nonsense before, even during her university races in the past.

Don't listen to it, she told herself and began counting, and then running through the alphabet to drown out the pain searing through her joints.

She was slowing she knew, but it was just as well. She would be coming to the edge of the park soon and then she had to make a choice. Either the longer route by road or head out across the fields. Part of her wanted to stick to the road that she knew, but her head told her that it would be an extra two or three miles if she went that way and now her ankle was bothering her, she wasn't sure the extra distance was a good idea. The fields would be trickier though and with potentially more hazards to trip on.

She was nearing the end of the park. The road curved around to the right, but the fields stretched out directly in front of her. Thankfully they had not been ploughed up and the surface was still stubble. This decided it. She stood at the entrance to the first field and checked her watch. It was five twenty and she had made good time. She adjusted the rucksack on her shoulders as the bottle of water was beginning to thump against her shoulder blades. She had been running the majority of the way in the darkness, but now flicked on her head torch, knowing that to run in a dark field would be asking for trouble.

She had already twisted her ankle and she didn't want to break a leg.

The field had no gate, but the entrance was wide open and had been recently driven through. The rutted tyre marks dug deep into the red clay of the earth. Cathy looked down, her torch picking out the furrowed cuts like slices of fudge icing. Her stomach suddenly gnawed like a knife twisting. It wasn't cramp, just a gut spasm. She grimaced in pain and wondered if she might vomit, but it passed and she limped on, stepping out onto the more level ground and getting a feel for the stubbled straw beneath her feet. Unsure where the field gate at the far end might be, she took a straight line across, heading in the direction she assumed she should go, using the drills that the farmer had sculpted with his combine. The stubble whipped cruelly at her ankles and crunched like ice beneath her trainers, but it was level and not too soft.

Behind her, the sun was beginning to rise. The clouds caught at the edges with a hint of purple and it wouldn't be long until the raw orange jolted the morning into life and people woke. Feeling as if she was being chased, she picked up her pace once more.

The first field was slippery in places. Her head torch helped guide her a good deal though and she managed to negotiate the length of the land without injuring herself. She came to the end of the field and looked for a gate, allowing herself to walk up the hedge until she found the gap in the shadows. She stopped, hands on hips, panting and bent over to stretch. A flap and a shrill shriek made her jump in terror as she disturbed a roosting pheasant. The bird panicked and fretted from the undergrowth, flailing awkwardly by her feet until it found its wings and became airborne. She cursed and rotated her ankle, allowing the joint to click. She bent over and felt the bone. It was beginning to swell up already, but she'd have to deal with that when she was finished.

Cathy crossed into the next field, another stubble and far larger. Beyond it, she knew would be two others at least until she came to the road once more. More tentatively than before, she set off, at times jogging, and at other times, having to half-hobble, half-walk. Between the second and third fields, she was met by a thick line of hedge with apparently no gate on that side. She made a couple of half-hearted attempts to push through and then, in growing frustration, plunged deep into the prickly foliage. On the other side, she found a ditch and a dense crop of brambles. She swore loudly, panic rising in her throat. The thorns tore at her legs and she had to consciously make herself slow her breathing and gently unhook her leggings and rucksack. It took a good two minutes to free her clothing from the barbs. Her head torch caught the crimson on her hands and she knew that she must be bleeding, but now was not the time to think about it. A hot shower when she got home. It was that thought that distracted her enough to negotiate the next field without further issue.

She came to the wood at the far side and knew that this must join the base of the Ancrum Road. Again, a deep gully was carved out from the full length. There was no way she could cross it in one. A glow was beginning to creep from behind her and she knew that she had little time before the sun rose now. The pinky rays had already begun to send shadows like elongated caricatures out from everything they touched. Cathy looked up and down the ditch and finding the narrowest part, took a run and made a leap. Her hands scrabbled at the other side as she just made it, but grabbing on a crop of nettles, she allowed herself to slither painfully into the watery dyke. The mud was freezing and she was up to her ankles in it. Her shoes were completely submerged and even trying to lift a foot out, she found the clay sucking her back down. Tears of self-pity stung at her eyes. She swiped them away, smearing her cheeks and forehead with mud and blood. Cathy groped around at the edge of the trench for anything. She needed some purchase to pull herself free. Finally, finding a low hanging tree branch, she grasped it and hauled herself out. She sat spent and panting by the side. Oh God, why on earth had she come this way?

She paused there, and unzipping her rucksack, she took a deep draft from her water bottle. She struggled to swallow; her throat ached so much from the cold air. The liquid sat painfully in her throat as her gullet refused to allow it past. Instinctively she hammered at her chest, trying to force the drink to go down. The spasm eased and she took another smaller sip. She looked behind and saw she was still being pressed onwards by the chinks of light in the clouds.

She turned and ahead saw the looming network of trees that bordered Ancrum Road. Feeling that she had little choice other than to continue, she once again got up and brushed the loose leaves from her legs. She hadn't allowed herself to contemplate how she was going to get home and a flash of utter defeat filled her suddenly, but again she quashed it.

Keep moving and think later, she told herself, and finally with great relief felt the solid, hard tarmac beneath her muddied trainers once more. Nearly there.

She had come out onto Ancrum Road far further down than she had intended. She walked the final half a mile, knowing that to any motorists who passed her, she must look quite a sight. She only saw two cars though and neither slowed as they drove by. She was forced to sidestep into the trees as one car splashed far too close for comfort, sending leaves and gritty water spraying up at her. She watched the disappearing tail lights, snaking their convoluted route out of town.

The lodge house appeared from the tall trees, a dark

unyielding mass. She walked quickly now, aware that time was not on her side. She would need to focus and concentrate on the task at hand. Her breathing was shallow and her heart still hammered in her ears as she silently crossed by the gates to the mansion house. At best, if she was caught, she was trespassing. At worst, she was breaking and entering.

23

The gravel crunching beneath her feet seemed to be unspeakably loud in the otherwise still early morning. Although she thought she must be unheard, she cautiously stepped instead onto the lawn. It had been completely covered by fallen leaves since she was last here. She felt the damp rustle and slip of them as she crossed to the lodge. She had switched off her head torch for fear of attracting attention as she had passed through by the gates. Although the sun was rising, it was still languid in its ascent and the objects around her were unfathomable and shadowy. She crept along the side of the lodge, her hands fumbling against the harled brickwork. At times, her fingers dragged and caught on the stone. She had avoided the flower border this time and moved in the opposite direction, hoping that her own and the other person's footprints, might still be visible later. Inside first, and then look at the prints before leaving, she decided.

As she felt along and around the corner of the small house, the ground suddenly changed consistency. She made a half-step, and nearly fell as the earth seemed to disappear beneath her. She cried out and immediately stifled herself, having landed awkwardly on her already throbbing ankle. Almost at once, however, she felt herself again on a stable footing. She ignored the ankle.

If anything, the path now was easier. They had paved round the back, of course. She had forgotten seeing this the last time she had been. There had been a small area of stone slabs. Presumably the Steers might have set out a couple of garden chairs in the summer. That was if they had stayed. Feeling she was out of sight from the road and the drive now, Cathy turned on her head torch once more and allowed the shaft of light to fall across the tiny courtyard. It was bounded by the high wall that surrounded the entire mansion itself. Cathy saw that here, just as up at the big house, a thick crop of ivy had been allowed to take hold. Many of the leaves from the tall trees that bordered the drive seemed to have blown here. Some had caught on the ivy, but more had fallen and had created a deep triangular mound in the corner. There was no washing line, and not even a hosepipe to indicate that the place had been lived in recently.

As she turned, the torch reflected off the window. Cathy was blinded by the sudden flash of light on her retinas and she screwed her eyes in pain. Slowly opening them again, the garden if anything, seemed even darker. She tentatively felt along the first window ledge, trying to get an idea of how it might move. The wood was quite old and the paint had splintered and bubbled. She slipped an arm free from her rucksack and unzipping the main compartment, removed the chisel. She had no idea what she was doing, but she made a few hesitant stabs at the gap between the frame and the window itself. The wood seemed quite rotten and at last the chisel seemed to almost disappear into it. The sound of fissuring timber made her freeze but she couldn't stop now.

Her breath was irregular and the icy cloud that came from her lips almost misted her vision. She twisted the end of the chisel. The handle was smooth and slipped, sending the tool clattering to the ground with a metallic clang on the paving stones.

She stood still and waited. She heard a car engine. The noise came closer. Cathy froze, the blood rushed from her face, and she began to tremble. The car seemed to slow as it came level with the lodge. Cathy, now shaking uncontrollably, turned off the head torch and crouched against the wall. Surely, she could not have been seen. The car engine was still running but it sounded as if the car had halted. Cathy held her breath and waited, trying to listen for any sound. She was still squatted uncomfortably by the wall of the lodge, her body pressed against the cold stone of the wall. The intense pain in her knees and ankles made it impossible for her to remain like that and she slowly straightened. As she did so, she heard the swish as the car's wheels began to move. The driver was now accelerating past the gates. Cathy saw to her horror that there was a gap in the wall that she hadn't known about. It was a kind of narrow decorative window she supposed and it had potentially exposed her presence. From her position in the darkness, she watched the car's headlights shine through the opening in the brickwork. Had they seen her torchlight moving behind the wall and thought it odd? But surely not.

With the sound of the car engine growing ever distant, Cathy scrabbled around to find the chisel. Now that her eyes had grown more accustomed to the gloom of the garden, she thought it safer to pry open the window in the darkness. She set to work with increased determination and speed, slotting the blade of the chisel in the same spot and twisting and heaving at the handle with all of her strength. She repositioned the tool several times until she heard something inside the window splinter and snap. Then, in a sudden jolt, the frame had come free and the window, heavy in her hands, slid up an inch. The dry wood caught against the casing and screamed in protest, but undeterred and now desperate to be inside, Cathy forced the thing up, until finally, she was looking deep into the cavernous innards of the house itself.

The window was chest height. She looked around for something to stand on but seeing nothing and the window now precariously forced open, all she could do was take a run at it. She stepped back and then summoning the last of her energy, skipped forward and grabbed at the ledge, hauling herself up. Her ribs slammed hard against the cold stone and she was momentarily winded. She gasped in pain and then wriggled so that her hips took her body weight. The wooden edge cut into them and unceremoniously she slithered and then collapsed onto the floor inside. The drop was far less than she had expected and she lay there for a moment, breathing hard and mentally checking herself over. She had cracked a rib without a doubt. Every intake of breath was a sharp stab at her chest. She knew though that the adrenaline would see her through the first hour or so, and after a minute, she cautiously sat up and looked around the room in which she lay.

She knew already that it and all the others would be bare but the haunted, sinister feeling that she experienced came as a surprise. Getting to her feet, she glanced outside choosing quite deliberately to ignore any such feelings and be practical instead. It must surely be safe now to put on her torch again. Not wanting to creep about in the dark, she did so. The light was tremulous but as she moved from first the back room to the hallway, and then into the kitchen and pantry, she felt sick to her stomach. She sniffed and the pungent tang of disinfectant hung in the air.

Everything was gone. Not a single carpet or mat had been left. She even looked in the sink, not knowing what she might see, but this had been cleaned and the stainless steel reflected back at her. All of the walls were bare, leaving behind the holes where pictures had once been hung. Cathy crossed the hallway again, this time to the front of the house, to the room into which she had peered that night. The house was cold, presumably having not had any heating on for about a week now. She shivered.

The room at the front was empty, like all the other rooms. She stood, looking around herself in disbelief. How had they taken it all? It was as if the Steers' lives had been obliterated along with their lost belongings and deleted medical records. Within a day, the chair that had been just where she stood, the picture and the lamp, everything had gone. She tried to be methodical and to think with the mind of an intelligent person, but climbing the stairs to what had been two bedrooms, one en suite, she found it increasingly hard to be logical. One thing that did prove her sanity, she supposed, was the door to one of the bedrooms. The lock had clearly been forced and the edge of the wood was fractured from the impact. So, Mr Steer had been speaking the truth, it seemed. She fingered the splintered wood. How fortunate it might be to find a scrap of material caught, even a thread, but there was nothing.

Cathy wasn't sure what she had expected. If she had been honest, she had perhaps hoped to stumble upon a torn corner of paper with a name or a number on it that might lead her to the solution. She was disappointed though. Upstairs, it seemed that the bedroom in which she assumed Mrs Steer had slept, had been cleaned even more thoroughly. Since she had entered the house there had been an unmistakable smell of disinfectant, but upstairs the aroma of bleach seemed to fill and choke her nostrils with every breath. She examined everything, even crouching down to look at the floorboards, they were still slightly damp presumably from the deep clean and lack of ventilation thereafter, but there was nothing to find. No paper had been dropped in a corner and there was nothing to reward her efforts.

The realisation that it had all been in vain hit her with such force that she staggered backwards. She rested her forehead against the cold wallpaper of the bedroom. Oh God, what had she done? Through the window, the sun had risen. Its orangey tendrils extended, saturating the thin morning air. The fronds of light came like clawing fingers, reaching for the windowsill, nearer and nearer. When they touched, the room was ablaze with fire.

She descended the stairs in defeat and stood in the hallway, feeling quite lost. She had learned nothing, but the one question that troubled her more than anything was: why had they cleaned the place with bleach?

24

It could only really mean one thing, she knew. Mr, and or, Mrs Steer had been killed. The bleach that had infiltrated the floorboards of the bedroom in which Mrs Steer had slept that single evening, spoke volumes. Why else would they have doused the place in disinfectant? Why rip up all the soft furnishings, unless there had been something unspeakable to hide? Cathy imagined the blood seeping in through the wooden slats and the perpetrator's frantic and yet meticulous efforts to obliterate the evidence. Oh God, what horrific crime had been committed in that dreadful house? She had read about cases where, not knowing how else to dispose of a body, insane murderers had hacked at their victim, dismembering it into small pieces that were easier to conceal. Was that what had happened here too?

Cathy looked up the staircase one last time. The ghosts of the couple were not there. If anything, the place was devoid of energy or emotion. Cathy sighed, now knowing that she must somehow make her way home. A wave of self-pity swept over her and she tried to swallow, but a painful lump in her throat prevented it. She looked down at her legs, smattered in mud, her trainers too. She had left a trail of dirt around the house. She hadn't thought to remove her shoes when she had come in, but then, the people up at the mansion house would know someone had been inside as soon as they discovered the forced window. Hopefully, they'd think it was squatters or someone looking to do an impromptu break-in. They would probably laugh, knowing that the culprit would have left empty-handed and disappointed.

Almost reluctant to begin her journey home, Cathy lingered in the hallway. She opened the front door, unbolting the latch. She might quickly check the footprints again outside and see if they had any distinctive quality about them, but other than that, she thought she had done all she could. There was a horrible sense of finality about it all. She felt that she had failed. And then there was the actual business of how to get home. She looked at her watch. It was a quarter to seven. She was going to be late for work without a doubt. She hadn't been late in all her years of employment there. It was the last thing James and Euan needed. Cathy knew that there was no way she could return home the same way. She thought of the deep ditches she had crossed and the muddy fields. She would have to go by road, but her ankle wouldn't stand the six or seven miles. There would be a line of taxis by the railway station at this time in the morning. If she walked, it would take her maybe half an hour.

She crept along the flower bed in search for the footprint, but stooping, she thought she heard a distant car engine. Without waiting, she returned to the house and shut the front door once more. She couldn't be seen in the garden. The footprint would have to wait if it was still there. She left the hallway and crossed through to the kitchen. Her head torch was still on. There had to be something, anything surely. The people must have dropped or ripped a bag. In desperation, she looked again all around the room. And then, as she was reaching to check the last of the cupboards that she had already examined once, she froze. There had been the drone of a car engine but it had stopped.

Cathy knew that she had not been mistaken, but still she hoped that her mind was simply playing the game of frightening her, for that thrill of adrenaline. She didn't need that now though. She was exhausted and she had already had enough for a lifetime. Now, to her dismay, she heard a crunch. Then another, it came closer and she knew in that second that it was the sound of someone approaching up the front gravel path. Someone had seen her torchlight and had come to investigate. Why had she been so foolish as to go out of the front door to hunt for footprints? And then she remembered the door and the bolt. She hadn't locked it behind herself. With rising panic, she stood in the kitchen, waiting. There was a click.

'Mrs Steer?'

It was a man's voice. Cathy stood poised ready to run. Someone believed Mrs Steer was still alive. Had they seen Cathy and assumed it was her?

'Mrs Steer, stop this,' the voice came again, perhaps a lilt of eastern European, Cathy thought. Definitely not one of the brothers from the mansion house. Whoever it was, was standing in the hallway. Cathy heard what she assumed was the door to the living room being kicked open. Footsteps. Only one person. They were moving through the house looking for her. With what she considered amazing foresight, rather than dive straight out, she had silently closed the door to the kitchen so that the view directly from the front door would not take the entrant straight to her.

'Why this nonsense when it was agreed, Mrs Steer?' came

the man's voice, cajoling, coaxing her. 'We have the money, my dear. You know the deal. Hand it over.' He spoke with a drawl but Cathy knew from his tone that he was growing impatient.

She would have to be quick. The footsteps had stopped abruptly and she imagined the man listening. It was now or never. He must realise that the only place left to look was the kitchen. Trying to do so without making a sound, Cathy hooked a leg over the windowsill and straddled it. She barely had time to think about the drop before she had done it. The pain in her ankle made her almost faint, but knowing that she would have only one chance to creep around the front and escape before the person now in the house realised where she had gone, she hobbled to the corner. There was a car in the driveway, a blacked-out saloon.

Cathy turned and saw the metal gates that she must get to. They were only fifty yards from where she stood, but the distance seemed unimaginably vast. If only she could get to the road, she would be safe. Screwing her fists up in preparation, she made a dash for it and prayed that the person inside the lodge would not be looking out of a front window just as she ran. She crossed the gravel, limping and falling, and in her peripheral vision, she saw the front door, wide open. Then, from within the house, there was a roar of fury.

Cathy's heart was now hammering uncontrollably. She sprinted for the gate and began to run up the Ancrum Road. Her ankle was on fire. The pain was so intense that it almost drove her on faster as if she was trying to escape it also. She heard another shout and then the heavy thudding of steps behind her. Frantically, she turned and looked over her shoulder, but she couldn't see who was chasing her. Her vision was blurred by tears and grime. She knew that she couldn't stop now, and if she did, the whole thing would be over.

The road was wet and slippery with mud and fallen

autumnal leaves. A car's headlights suddenly appeared over the crest of the hill. A spray of slimy sludge and water scattered off of the wheels like a hiss. The car was travelling at some speed. Cathy staggered, not knowing whether to flag it down or keep on running. Her breath was laboured and she felt herself begin to stumble. The sound of the car engine and her blood thundered in her ears until it deafened her.

And then it happened in a disjointed slow-motion. She had been running into the line of traffic as she always did, but the car seemed only to see her at the last second. She saw the driver begin to slow and heard the screech and slip of tyres and brakes. Instinctively, Cathy leapt sideways. She heard a hoarse cry and wondered if it had come from her own throat. The car was so close. It was sliding like it was on ice. She looked up but didn't see the driver, just a reflection of her own pale, frightened face in the glass windscreen. She thought she heard the deep bellow of a man. The rest was a rubble of fragmented memories, like fragile shards of snapshots imprinted on cut-glass. There was an image of Dr Kidd. He was looking down at her. She couldn't understand where he had come from, but his face was covered in blood. He looked so distraught that she almost wanted to reach up and touch him. Then she heard another engine coming and tried to move. There was a pain in her side and she heard someone crying. Perhaps it was herself. When she opened her eyes again, there was no sound, only the rocking motion, and the impression of a flickering neon blue.

When she woke, it was with a start and at first, the clattering of a trolley passing the room and the beep of a machine by her bed didn't make any sense. She opened her eyes and although the room was dimly lit, she made out a clock on the wall. It was eleven thirty.

Morning or night? she wondered stupidly and smiled to herself. There was a smell of disinfectant that was very familiar and then in the same moment, she realised both where she was and why she was there. She sat up and was immediately forced to flop back again. The pain in her ribs was excruciating. She shifted her legs, trying to free them from the impossible blankets, but she was again met with a piercing stab and something bulky on her leg. Had she been run over? Suddenly she recalled Dr Kidd's face, so full of alarm and what else had been in his eyes? Was it guilt? Guilt for what? For running her down? Had he been the driver? And then she thought of the person chasing her. Maybe it had been Dr Kidd chasing her all along.

By the time the nurse came to administer her pain medication some ten minutes later, Cathy was confused but determined. Whatever happened now, she must be very careful with what she said. She didn't know who she could trust.

'And how are you feeling?' the nurse asked, moving to the window to pull up the blind. It turned out that it was still morning and Cathy had only been in the hospital bed for a matter of two hours.

'All right, I suppose,' she said. 'Was I hit by a car?'

'Nearly, it seems, but thankfully not, although you've somehow fractured two ribs and torn the ligaments in your ankle.'

'Torn ligaments?' Cathy asked in disbelief, remembering how she had still run on it. 'What about the man in the car. He tried to brake. I was out running.'

'I don't know about him. It's you I've been thinking about,' the nurse said. 'If he came in, he's not on our ward. I can only assume that if he didn't hit you, he was all right.'

Cathy took the small plastic cup of tablets from her.

'Co-codamol and diclofenac,' the nurse replied to her raised eyebrow. 'You'll be starting to get sore again soon. Listen, Cathy. I'm sorry to have to ask this, but was there a reason you were running away? The doctors... I mean, the staff in A&E cleaned you up before you came to the ward, but you've been in the wars. Covered in bruises and scratches all over. I'm sorry to be blunt, but has anyone done this to you? Were you running away from anyone? We must know now. The police, you see? They should be informed if there's any question of it.'

Cathy's eyes grew wide with terror. 'No,' she stammered. 'No one was chasing me. I was jogging and I fell.'

The nurse nodded, but it was clear she didn't believe her. She moved to the door. 'Do you want us to contact anyone? I think someone had already phoned your work. You're a GP, I believe? Glainkirk Practice?'

'Yes, but...'

The nurse raised a hand to quieten her. 'Rest up for a couple of hours,' she suggested. 'I don't know what happened, but you've been through the wars. I'll be popping in and out to check on you. If you need anything at all, buzz and I'll come. We thought it better to give you a side room. Privacy in case something else had... Well, I'm glad you're looking brighter now at least.' The nurse was almost out the door when she turned and as an afterthought: 'Oh, we've had a few concerned people on the phone asking for you already. A Dr Kidd. He said he was a GP at your practice. Wanted to know about your condition. I think he said he was planning to come in this afternoon after he had finished consulting himself. Very concerned for you,' she said, smiling. 'Anyway, you get some sleep so you're fresh and able to chat with your colleagues later.'

Cathy smiled back but felt anything but cheerful. As the door swung shut, she knew she couldn't be here when Stuart

Kidd came. She had to get as far away from the place as she possibly could. As the nurse had spoken, it had begun to fall into place. Dr Kidd was the murderer and now she wondered if the car accident hadn't been so accidental after all. She recalled the screech of brakes, but the car's course hadn't altered. Had Dr Kidd intended to kill her also?

25

Cathy felt that the bedrock of her life had shifted and cracked. Everything that she had believed in was no longer true. She had always trusted in the system, in the police, in her colleagues as doctors. She had gone into this career with altruism. She took for granted that her colleagues felt the same way. How was it that Dr Kidd had veered so terribly from that course? How could he become so manipulated and alien to the practitioner he had once been? Cathy recalled the hours sitting in his consulting room. She had openly wept in front of the man, desperate to return to work herself and at the time, had been so hopelessly far from being able to do so. He had consoled her; he had gone out of his way to chase up psychiatric appointments for her and had even told her that day or night he was contactable. But the narrative that she thought was true, had been broken. There was nothing to replace it but doubt and fear.

'I need to get away,' she said to the empty room.

It was only as she began to shift, easing her legs out of bed, finding her left ankle encased in a tight Tubigrip bandage, that she realised how difficult it would be. There would be a line of taxis at the rank outside the hospital, though. Cathy dressed, finding her muddied but thankfully dry clothes in a plastic bag by her bed, and somehow, she limped out of the ward without notice. Everyone was so busy, they had enough on their own plates without keeping track of potential escapees. Every movement seemed to be like a new assault on her body. She discovered pain where she had not known it before. Interestingly, despite the ankle, it was in fact a juicy blister on the side of her foot that was causing the greatest issue for her. By the time she reached the door to the hospital, she was completely exhausted and frustrated by her slow progress. But at least she was there now.

A car drove forward, cutting the queue and Cathy got in. The driver was large and jovial, and when he asked where she wanted him to take her, she hesitated. Not home. That would surely be the first place they might look. Whoever they might be. There was Suzalinna's of course, but then that must surely be the next place anyone who knew her would hunt. With the kind of tired resignation that can only come through defeat, she asked him to take her to Westfield.

'Whereabouts in Westfield are we heading?' the man asked conversationally as he signalled and drove. 'I could take a couple of routes, but it depends which part of town you're after.'

Cathy told him. She wasn't sure what kind of reception she would get from Chris but she had little choice.

The journey seemed to take an age. The driver took a back road and Cathy began to feel anxious as lane after country lane passed by, none of which she recognised.

'Not been well?' the driver asked out of interest.

'Just an accident,' she said. 'I fell out running.'

He nodded and chuckled. 'Never went in for any of that kind of nonsense myself. And there you are, I was right to ignore my doctor's advice about getting fit. Only ends you up in hospital.'

Cathy smiled and looked out of the window once more. They continued in silence for some minutes. 'Are you sure this is the way?' she asked eventually.

The man laughed. 'The right way? Yes, we're coming in through the back route. I know the roads like the back of my hand,' he said. 'I grew up on the other side of Westfield.'

Unhappily, Cathy watched field after field pass by as they continued. It had been too long though. She looked at her watch. They had been driving for nearly fifteen minutes now. She was about to ask him to stop and let her out when at last the spire of Westfield's church came into sight and she sighed, having been holding her breath for goodness knows how long.

It was a relief to be out of the cab. She paid the grinning cab driver. He charged far too much for his trouble, but she would have handed over three times as much. She almost fell up the steps to Chris's house. By then, the taxi had disappeared into the distance and she stood alone and shivering, not sure what he would say, or how he would look. Her heart hammered as the door was opened and he stood there. He seemed overcome with emotion at first. Cathy had never seen him look that way. When he spoke, the words came out like bullets.

'Jesus Christ! What happened?' He had changed. Even in the last month. His face looked more angular, and he was no longer clean-shaven. A shadow of hair, not quite a beard but near-enough, covered his jaw. He looked up the street and then back at her. 'Jesus,' he swore again. 'Get inside now. What the hell happened?' He looked angry and she couldn't tell if it was at her.

Cathy stood in the hallway and ran a hand through her hair. It was damp and her fingers snagged on the knots. She was so beaten, it was all she could do to stay upright. He had shut the door behind her, slamming it so that the snib clicked into place itself. The hallway was too bright and she squinted and blinked, her eyes already full of tears anyway. She knew his house so well and yet she saw that it had changed. He had hung a new mirror and had moved the table that had always been there to toss her car keys onto after a long day. She looked down at her feet, aware that she had dragged mud and water onto the polished wooden floors.

'Oh, don't bother,' he said distractedly. 'For God's sake, come through and sit down. You were the last person I expected to see.'

He didn't touch her but led the way through, pacing like an incensed cat. The living room was as she remembered. He tugged the thick, tartan throw that she had given him as a gift, from the back of the sofa and wrapped it over her shoulders. She hadn't realised how badly she was shaking. Now her whole body seemed to have lost control and she was crying and trembling and unable to say a thing.

He swore and left the room. Perhaps she shouldn't have come at all.

He was in the kitchen. The kettle was boiling and she heard the clink of glass. She sat huddled, trying to pull herself together because she knew he'd have questions for her soon enough and she'd have to explain.

When he returned, he seemed to have more restraint. He handed her a hot water bottle. It was hers. She recognised the cover. She had held it tight into her abdomen before. She took it and did the same, wrapping herself around its heat, trying to press the warmth from it into her fingers and her core. He had brought her a drink. He placed it on the table in front of her.

'It's whisky. I know you hate the stuff, but it's all I had.'

She hardly heard him, but she released a hand and put the beaker to her lips. She was trembling so much that the glass rattled against her top teeth. She gulped. It was excruciating and burned at her throat. She grimaced and then laughed.

'Better?' he asked and she nodded.

Yes. That was better, and slowly she began to warm up. He turned on the gas fire and the orange flame convoluted and flicked until it settled to a steady glow. Gradually, she felt her shoulders aching and she knew that she must be more relaxed. All this time, he sat pensively, watching her, but not saying a word. Perhaps there were none.

She didn't know where to begin herself. When she did speak, her voice was quite level. 'I'm being followed.'

He met her gaze and she wondered what his expression meant. She used to know him so well but perhaps even that had changed.

'Really,' she reiterated, thinking that it must be disbelief. 'They've taken two people and I'm next. If you don't believe me, then God knows... Chris. I need...' but she tailed off, because how could she ask him? They had once been a team, but now they were quite separate entities. Even voicing it aloud made her doubt herself.

Finally, he spoke. 'Cathy...' He shook his head and got up sharply and began walking to and fro, across the hearth rug, back and forth. She watched him impassively. He didn't believe her. She couldn't blame him. It had been a mistake coming. He stopped and turned. 'Your medication?' he asked, spitting the words out.

She swallowed. Her mouth was dry and her throat ached as if something painful was lodged there. Her medication... She hadn't taken it for days it was true, but that didn't alter things.

'Why does it always come back to that?' she managed.

'How dare you?' he said quietly, but his voice was shaking. 'How dare you? You turn up on my doorstep, looking like this. You scare the life out of me. It's been four weeks. Four weeks, Cathy. Not a word and you expect me to bail you out of the next drama? Yes, I ask about the tablets. Of course, I bloody ask. I lived through the bipolar with you. It was my life too.'

'I thought you understood...' she began and then stopped. Her throat was raw and she couldn't find the words anyway.

'I've waited for you to call. It was like I was being punished and I didn't know why.' His voice was anguished like he was saying something he had rehearsed in his head but the words were all wrong. 'Were you punishing me? What did I do? I still don't know, not even now. I go into work and every time my bleep goes for an outside line, I think it's you. At home, I've waited...'

She hesitated, just long enough for him to make a noise of disgust.

'Chris, please...' she began, but she didn't know how to make it right. Her eyes shifted and faltered from his gaze, which was so full of hurt and anger it made it impossible to go on. She looked down at her hands, still covered in fresh grazes and scuffs of mud. In her head, she had been the victim, the one to suffer both the bipolar and then the miscarriage. He hadn't understood the toll it had taken on her. He hadn't been strong enough to stay, to offer her the security that she so desperately wanted. She hadn't thought about him. Not once, if she was honest.

He was at the door now and he turned, his face twisted with emotion. 'You can stay. Sort yourself out, whatever, but I can't... you know. I just can't, if you keep lying to yourself. I know it's the illness, but...'

'Chris, no,' she said desperately. 'No, please.' She got up. The tartan blanket fell to the floor. She tried to move between him and the door. 'Please, you have to believe me. People are dying. Two people are dead and I'm next. It's Dr Kidd, my own GP. He's the murderer.' She reached out a hand.

'Get off me,' he said gruffly and pushed past her. It was the first time since she had arrived that he had touched her and she fell back, crying out in pain. He hesitated, clearly regretting it, but as she gasped and held her side, he headed for the stairs.

'Suzalinna's pregnant,' she called out after him, her voice cracking, and for a moment he stopped, his foot on the first step. He didn't turn, but she knew he was close to crying and she couldn't bear to look. 'Chris, please,' she begged, but slowly he began to climb the stairs.

She sat on the bottom step growing cold and sore, trying to muffle the sound of her sobs.

26

He went out that night. He wasn't on call because he didn't have his hospital badge. She had been dozing on the sofa all afternoon, not daring to go upstairs to wash or to speak to him. He looked in before leaving. She saw his reflection in the glass of the fire, but lay still, pretending she was asleep. Silently, he laid a towel and a dressing gown on one of the chairs, alongside it, a toothbrush still in its packet. More than anything she wanted to talk, but she knew he had been right in what he said. When she heard the door quietly close, she lay for a further five minutes, shifting her position and wondering how she would make it up the stairs. A shower would undoubtedly make her feel more human, though.

She stood in his en suite bathroom. Shocked by her gaunt reflection, she turned away and switched on the shower. Slowly, she peeled off her clothes and with some difficulty, the Tubigrip on her ankle also. The shower took ages to run hot. It always had done. She stood impatiently and then reaching out a hand to check the temperature, winced as the water ran over her grazed fingers. The water was both invigorating and painful. She lathered herself with soap, allowing the steam to rise and encircle her. Her ankle had stiffened up considerably already, but the hot water on it helped. She watched idly as the water eddied and pooled at the plug. Initially, it ran a brownish red as the mud and grit from her ordeal, intermingled with the blood from her scratches and scrapes, disappeared. When she was done, she patted herself dry, too sore to dry herself fully, and wrapped the dressing gown that smelled of him around her. The sleeves were too long and she folded them up over her wrists.

She waited, not wanting to take anything without his say-so, but when it got to eight o'clock, she realised she'd be spending the evening alone. She ate supper eventually, taking the minimum from the fridge and making herself scrambled eggs. Tired of her own company and half-afraid of the silence, she pulled the curtains in the living room and turned on the television. She would sleep on the sofa. She had already looked into the spare room and the bed had been made up, but she couldn't bring herself to go upstairs again and anyway, the sofa seemed more temporary, a more casual arrangement.

She lay in the growing darkness, with the flickering pictures from the TV casting shadows up the walls around her, not knowing what she was going to do. She couldn't stay here forever. Chris was angry and she didn't blame him. He didn't believe a thing she said. Even she knew that the story of Dr Kidd following her, of the missing patients, and the empty house, sounded utterly fantastical. Anyone who knew her might assume that she was suffering from a bipolar crisis. She was hypomanic with the telltale paranoia that she had suffered in the past, this time coupled with impossible delusions. The horrible truth was that she couldn't even deny that she had become erratic in taking her medication. These past few weeks due to her increased workload with Euan taking time off and her worries over James's retirement, her daily patterns had become unpredictable. She thought of the foil packet of tablets that sat in her bathroom and couldn't even remember when she last took one. *Oh God, what a mess.*

She tried to settle herself down on the sofa once more. This time though, the cushions cut into her back and the blanket slipped too far down. She must speak to Chris when he came home. She needed to apologise and to explain her behaviour. As the hours passed though, it became clear that he wasn't coming home that night. It was one thirty when she finally switched off the television, and even later when she cried herself to sleep.

When the morning came, she felt quite different. Where he had stayed last night, she didn't know. She had tortured herself the previous evening imagining him in the arms of a new girlfriend, of the two of them sitting on her sofa, flicking the channels and drinking wine. But the cold light of day, made her reconsider and she knew from his reaction when she had arrived the day before, that he hadn't moved on at all. Neither of them had.

It was seven o'clock when she heard the sound of a key in the lock. Her heart was in her throat instantly and she hastily folded the tartan throw and repositioned the cushions on the sofa, plumping them beside her where she sat.

He was in the doorway and it was blatantly clear that he had been drinking heavily. His trousers were creased and his face flushed. His mouth hung slack and his eyes looked raw. He had an expression of resigned defeat. It was as if he was in utter despair. Neither of them spoke. Him, perhaps not trusting the words due to the alcohol, and her, due to her sobriety. She needed to apologise but didn't know where to begin.

'I was worried,' she said, and instantly knew she had said the wrong thing.

He turned on his heel and headed to the kitchen, within moments, banging and dropping a pan. Cathy listened from the living room, but unable to stand it any longer, she got up and went through.

'I'm sorry. Really. Everything. I'm so sorry. I should have talked. I just couldn't.'

He turned his face towards her and his expression was filled with hopelessness. She knew that more than anything he wanted to believe her, to believe that she could care enough about herself, about him, to take her tablets and to be well.

'I can't make any promises...' she began and he looked down at his feet. 'It makes me selfish, the bipolar. I know that. I don't think. More than anything, I didn't want to hurt you. You were everything. You still are...'

He didn't look at her but stood propped awkwardly against the kitchen cupboards, too hung-over to stand himself. His face, full of suffering.

'Chris?'

He looked up at her and his eyes were almost pleading. Cathy felt suddenly sick.

'Chris, you have to believe me. I can't tell you I've taken my medication because I haven't. I hold my hands up. But what I said yesterday... I know it sounded crazy. I know all that. But please. You were the only one I could come to. Out of everyone; James, Euan, even Suzalinna, it was you I trusted to help me. I don't deserve your friendship after everything, but... Oh God, I don't even know where to begin.'

She didn't cry, knowing he would assume it was self-pity. She had no tears left anymore anyway.

He wobbled free of the countertop.

'I need to shower.' He staggered slightly in the doorway but turned. 'The apology,' he said. 'Yes. I needed to hear it. It's a shame you waited until you were desperate though.'

'That's not why...' she began and her words were beseeching. 'I mean it whether you help me or not, Chris...'

He left her standing in the kitchen, her fingers wrapped tightly around the worktop edge until the line was so indented on her palm that when she removed her grip, it left a deep depression. She had blown it, she knew. While she listened to him clumsily undressing, stumbling and banging, then the shower switching on, she tried to think. Where could she go now? In some ways, she was surprised that she hadn't been traced to his house. Every time a car engine slowed outside, she found herself holding her breath. She knew that James would be worried. How they were managing to cover her surgeries too, was something that concerned her, but to contact work would only lead to her detection and she knew that at all costs she must lie low.

It was a further hour until he came downstairs. He had sobered up but his eyes were still bloodshot and painfully sad. She made him coffee while he looked out of the kitchen window, lost in some kind of trance. She sat at the table watching him drink the scalding dark liquid, wondering how they had come to this, remembering how it had once been.

They had argued often enough during their relationship. They had squabbled like any other couple. Just silly things at first. Sometimes it had been about either of them working late. He was doing extra shifts at the hospital and at times it had seemed that he was the most eager on the surgical team to step in when one needed covering at the last minute. When Cathy had found out she was pregnant though, the arguments had stopped. Perhaps the stakes were higher and they knew then that the small stuff didn't matter, couldn't matter, anymore. They had to pull as a team from now on, to let the little things go. It had been unconscious on her part. She had been so happy at the time, so full of anticipation and hope. And then everything had changed. She had struggled to talk afterwards. She had assumed that he hadn't cared as much and she created a narrative in her head that he had been relieved that she had lost the baby. In the early hours of the morning, she even convinced herself that he blamed her. She became bitter. Her head was full of injustice and spite. She felt she had been tricked into believing that she deserved a happy ending and it had all been a lie. The whole thing had been a lie.

They both began to distance themselves from one another. He had taken to coming to bed an hour later, saying that he couldn't sleep as early as she could.

She knew that he was drinking after she went up: she could smell the bitterness on his breath despite his attempts to conceal it. She listened as he padded through to the kitchen, quietly opening the cupboard door. In the morning she saw that he had washed and replaced the glass, rather than leaving it on the sink top as he did with all of the other plates and mugs.

He knew as well as she did that for a surgeon to arrive at work in anything other than a sober and fresh state was tantamount to malpractice. But if he had used alcohol to numb the situation, she had tried to find solace in her work. She had taken on more shifts at the out-of-hours service. She had begun to stay back, putting off the inevitable return home, the forced civility and the inability to address the enormous issue that clung like a damp vapour in the air wherever she went. She despised herself for it.

As she sat at the table, knowing that they needed to talk, she wished she could explain it to him. She was exhausted with the assumptions and the expectations both of them had placed on one another. The split had done nothing. It hadn't healed anything for either of them. They were both still two separate edges of a wound. Where had it gone so wrong? What had been filled with promise and optimism, was now an unhealed scar. It had scabbed over but the tissue was too fragile to hold. Did he still love her? She wanted to ask him outright, but she didn't have a claim to that kind of information. Not anymore. She closed her eyes and leaning her elbows on the table, rubbed the heels of her hands into the sockets, feeling the gritty sleep shift. Oh God, what a mess.

They were still sitting in silence when there was a knock at the door. Cathy's breath caught and she froze in absolute terror.

'Don't tell them I'm here,' she hissed.

He looked confused and began to get up.

'Honestly, Chris, if you have anything left for me, anything, please do this. Don't tell them. Please.' She was begging, but she was desperate. She crept around the back of the kitchen table, standing with her back to a cupboard door. She was shaking. She knew it was them. Of course, they had come. 'Answer it, but don't say anything. You've not seen me, not in months,' she hissed again.

He moved to the door and she searched his face, looking for affirmation. He nodded slightly and shut the kitchen door.

She heard voices, but she stayed crouched where she was, willing Chris to play his part, for him to deny having ever seen her since the split. Above anything else, he couldn't let them in. She thought of the living room door. Had it been open? There was the tartan throw, half-folded, and the cushions propped up on the sofa as a pillow. Would they guess he had had a visitor if they saw? And who were 'they' anyway? Was Dr Kidd one of them? She still didn't know; or why they had killed the Steers. She held her breath and listened.

The voices rose and fell. Two men, she thought, but couldn't be sure. Chris was laughing. It was half-hearted as if he was playing it cool.

Get rid of them. Tell them to go, that you're hung-over, or busy, or anything.

Eventually, she heard the front door close. She listened to

the footsteps as they approached the kitchen door, still holding her breath. It was just one person though. Chris came in.

'Okay,' he said. 'We do need to talk. That was the police looking for you. James was concerned. Start at the beginning and tell me.'

They sat for over an hour. As she spoke, he made another coffee for them both, he made toast too and forced her to eat two slices. The story came in dribs and drabs and she knew that she didn't tell it well. Slowly her narrative began to falter and finish. He interrupted and asked questions. She tried to respond but some of the answers, even she didn't know. She implored him to believe her. It might well be that she was tipping into hypomania, even she admitted that, but this had happened. All of it. When she finished, she studied him, waiting for his reply. He looked tired but eventually, he nodded.

'Chris...' she began. She wanted to ask where this left them. He knew what she was going to say though and he shook his head.

'I'll help,' he said. 'The rest though... I can't say...'

She held her breath for a long time, looking down at the toast, swimming in butter that he had spread for her. What he had offered was all that she could ask.

27

'So, they'd returned from India?' Chris said. 'Do you think she was unwell then or was it an excuse to get out of the house and away from him?'

'Her husband? But why? Why not just do so, or not get on the plane at all? If she hated him that much, why did she go out there in the first place? And then, if the marriage was still bad, why return? She had no family here.'

'The other man? He was the draw back to Scotland surely.'

Cathy sighed. Yes, there was that. 'I had thought it was Dr Kidd but now I wonder if it was one of his brothers. That horrible man I met at the mansion house, Archie. I don't think it was him. He mentioned having a wife himself, although he didn't speak too highly about her either, he spoke about another brother too. Maybe Eddie and Mrs Steer had been carrying on. If there had been a dreadful family feud, there would be no love lost if he did take up with his brother's wife. What about this eastern European man who was looking for her? He sounded very angry. I wonder what he meant about handing over the money to her. Was she involved with some criminal gang and things got out of control?' Cathy sighed. 'But if they had taken her, why then did they think it was her in the lodge house that night? None of it makes sense.'

Chris rubbed his neck. 'I can't understand that bit either, but let's just say she came back to complete this criminal deal or to see her lover.' Chris spread his hands wide. 'Well, then what?'

'I can only assume that her husband got wind of it and decided to kill her,' Cathy said unhappily, not liking the solution at all.

'It doesn't sit well though, does it?' he said. 'Where did the husband go then? Did he disappear because you began poking around? Why come to you in the first place, if he didn't want to stir things up?'

'I'm assuming the eastern Europeans are out of the running. They still think Mrs Steer alive so they can't be that deeply involved.' Cathy sighed and folded her arms. 'Okay, well how about the Steer family, or the lover? Did they realise what Mr Steer had done and to avenge her death, or to avoid a family scandal, got rid of him too? They cleaned up the house and paid someone to remove the medical records too. They are a powerful family. It would be quite possible.'

'It doesn't sound plausible and I don't like there being two murderers,' he said shaking his head, 'but the bleach is worrying. Why clear out the house so thoroughly unless there was something horrible done there? I wonder what happened to the bodies. Could they have buried them on the estate? Was there disturbed earth, or anything when you were falling about the place?'

Cathy snorted. 'Not that I saw, but I was hardly able to look. Perhaps burying them on site would have been foolish though.'

'Where else then? I know the council tip's on the Ancrum Road but they could hardly dispose of two bodies without being seen, and in the middle of the night.'

Cathy shook her head. 'Where would you bury them then?'

He thought and then a smile crept to his lips. 'Well, obviously the best place to hide a body, or two, is in a graveyard.'

He laughed but Cathy remained silent, still thinking. She turned to him, with a new light in her eyes.

'Chris, you know, you could be right.'

'Looks like a funeral just now,' Chris said as he pulled into the lay-by at the top of the hill. 'Maybe we should stay put for a bit and wait until they're done.'

Cathy had been jumpy the whole way in the car, fearing that they might be being followed.

'No one's watching us,' he said as she spun in her seat, following the path of a car as it rounded the corner of the hill. The car indicated and drove into the gates of the high-walled cemetery. They had come to the top of Westfield Hill. God knows why the church had been built up here. It was windswept and the leaves from the trees surrounding the place whipped against the windscreen of the car in sudden gusts, making Cathy flinch.

Chris looked across at her. 'I wish you'd let me drive to your house.'

'The tablets, you mean? Don't keep on about it,' she said. 'Another day won't make a bit of difference as you well know. I told you the house will be under surveillance. There's no way you'd get in and out and not be followed straight back to me.'

He sighed. 'It all seems too impossible. What are we going to do when we go in anyway?'

Cathy peered out of the window. A thin rain had begun to come on and the drops fell like slashes on the glass. She stared through the gates at the gaggle of black-coated mourners just inside, their outline distorted by the rain. Umbrellas were hastily being put up now to shield them from the elements. Above, the clouds were thick and menacing, with the promise of a far heavier downpour by the looks of things.

'I suppose, look for a recently dug grave,' she said.

The minister had come into view, a stooping elderly man. They sat in silence and watched him. His black robe caught in the wind and fretted at his legs. He spoke to the group of mourners and then led the way to the little grey church that stood hunched against the high wall of the cemetery.

'If it is here – the body, I mean – it suggests that they are all corrupt. The minister would have to have been involved too in some way,' Chris said.

'Yes and no,' she replied without turning. 'He'd have been paid not to ask questions about the hurried funeral, but he wouldn't need to know the details.' Cathy had worried about the number of individuals that seemed to have become embroiled in the deaths of Mr and Mrs Steer. A good deal of money must have been spent to keep the thing quiet. It did seem to point in one direction only. It had to be that of the family. She looked out as the last of the mourners moved into the shelter of the church. 'Do you think now that they've gone in...?' she asked.

Chris shrugged. It was obvious that he didn't want to get out of the car at all, let alone be there. She looked at him pleadingly and he nodded. Together they unlocked their doors. Cathy zipped the jacket, fastening it tight around her throat. It was one of his and was enormous on her. The wind took full advantage and forced its way under. Cathy plunged her hands deep into the pockets, drawing the folds of the coat firmly around her, trying to stop the chill, but could not prevent herself from shaking. She wondered if that was from the cold at all, though. Chris was beside her. He rested a hand lightly on her shoulder. She felt every finger, despite the heavy quilt of the jacket she wore.

'Come on then, let's get it over with.'

He set out, his stride far longer than hers so that she had to stumble and jog to keep up. Her ankle was now bandaged properly and this, in combination with the over-the-counter analgesia that he had in the house, seemed to be enough to keep her from any real discomfort. He slowed as he came in line with the gates. When she caught up, she saw that the church at the far side was lit. Directly outside the building, two long black cars were parked. One was a hearse. Although the mourners had disappeared, a man, probably employed by the funeral directors, hovered by the door, perhaps in case of latecomers. He looked across at them and Chris raised a hand, indicating that they weren't there for the service. The man nodded and turned away.

'Well?' he asked. 'It looks a bit weird us marching up and down all the graves now that he's seen us. He'll be thinking we're mad. We should know where the grave of our loved one is if that's what we're doing.'

Cathy knew he was right. She scanned the graveyard. 'Turn and look like we're in conversation,' she hissed.

'We are. I don't need to bloody pretend.'

She raised her eyebrows in a scathing grimace. 'Listen. Let's be a bit clever. If it was a quickie funeral and done on the quiet, they'd hardly choose a plot up here by the gate where all these big headstones are. It would be more private.' They both looked to the left. Some of the stonework was quite ornate and ostentatious. 'Nothing like that,' Cathy said, nodding slightly.

'No, I suppose you're right,' he agreed. 'The plot would be secluded and the headstone unclear, or at least insignificant. What if it's a false name?' he suddenly asked.

Cathy shook her head. 'Jesus Chris. Don't make it even harder for us. We'll cross that bridge when we come to it. Come on. I think down by those trees.'

She linked her arm into his, more out of pretence for the benefit of the man by the church door than anything else. He wasn't looking though, but Cathy left her hand in the crook of his arm, liking the closeness. They walked slowly, both of them looking on either side, left and right.

'I guess the grass would have been relaid,' he said. 'How long ago, do you think it happened?'

'No more than fourteen days. Nothing along here. Let's turn down the way.' They followed the damp path, their shoes crunching on the loose grit. 'Look mournful or something in case that man's watching us,' she said.

'He's smoking a cigarette,' Chris scoffed. 'I don't think he cares what we're doing.'

They came to a fork in the path.

'Will we separate to make it quicker? The chances are this is a wild goose chase anyway,' he said, shuffling his feet in a puddle and drawing the collar of his jacket up against a forceful gust of rain and wind.

'Okay,' she agreed, now unwilling to let go of his arm. 'You go along there then, and I'll head up here. For God's sake don't make a big fuss if you do think you've found it though.'

He gave her a look as if she was telling him something very obvious indeed.

'Good luck,' she hissed, barely knowing why she continued to whisper. The man was quite far away and clearly occupied with kicking at the tyres of the hearse. She moved as quickly as she dared, her eyes sweeping up and down the lines of gravestones, looking for any changes in the ground; any evidence at all that it had been recently cut and moved. She was soon nearing the bottom of the cemetery. She turned and saw Chris. He had made faster progress and was now quite far in the distance, not quite lost to sight in the sea of grey headstones. He seemed to sense her eyes on him and he turned and raised a hand. Did that mean he had found something or was he just waving? Cathy cursed herself for not being clearer in her instructions at the beginning. She stood watching as he turned away and then immediately, he looked back at her. He must have found something. He wasn't moving on and was standing quite still in the same place.

Cathy crossed to a path that would lead her to him. The grey quarry dust scattered and crunched beneath her feet as she approached. In places, she had to sidestep to avoid a puddle. She was fifty yards from him and he still hadn't moved. As she drew nearer, she could see why. The grass had indeed been placed carefully back so that the earth was not showing, but the grave in front of Chris had been recently dug. A line was cut deep into the turf surrounding the area and the ground itself was slightly higher as if it had recently been dug and the excess earth put back in on top. She came nearer, her breath shallow and her heart racing.

'The name?' she asked.

His body had been blocking where the headstone must be, but as he moved to the side, she could see for herself. It hit her like a slap of icy water, knocking the breath out of her. She felt herself falling into an abyss of confusion and uncertainty. She knew he was looking at her, but she couldn't speak.

'Cathy?' he sounded unsure. 'We were being stupid, Cathy. Of course, it wouldn't be here.'

She stared up at him, her eyes glazed and wide.

'No, honestly. This is normal,' he said, half-laughing now at her. 'Two weeks ago, you said, wasn't it? They'd not have had it engraved yet. That's why there's no stone. My God, you went sheet white. We'll find the sexton. He'll know the name surely, or the minister when he's finished. That'll be the only way.'

Cathy realised that her fists had been clenched and she released them. Still, she didn't speak.

'Cathy,' he said softly. 'If this is it, we'll get you your name, okay? But please prepare yourself. Plenty of other people may have been buried in the last couple of weeks. This might not be the one. We'll go back to the car.'

In the distance, she could hear voices, as the mourners had begun to emerge from the little grey church.

'Let's not watch,' he said and guided her back along the gravelled path.

She sat in silence. He'd turned the heating on and the fan was aimed at her hands. The tips of her fingers had gone white, but she didn't notice. Was she finally a step closer to finding the final resting place of Mr or Mrs Steer? But more than that, was she going to find the reason that they had disappeared so suddenly? And if it did turn out that she was right, what happened then? If the minister said that the grave belonged to Mrs Steer, what could she do?

28

Her ankle was throbbing again and as they sat and waited for the last of the mourners to leave the graveside, Cathy tried to massage some of the swelling down. The ribbing of her sock had left a deep indentation in the skin.

Now that it had been over twenty-four hours since she had twisted it, a mottled purple had appeared. It showed that the blood under the skin had tracked with gravity. Some of the shade had spread as far as her heel now. Cathy had always found her patients fixated on their own bruising, describing with graphic detail the change in colours that their injured limb had gone through. It was the body's natural response to injury. There would be a short internal bleed which would result in the discolouration of the bruise, but as the blood became gradually reabsorbed again by the tissues, this would lead to the myriad of rainbow hues across the skin.

'You shouldn't be on your feet as much,' Chris said. 'It'll be like a balloon when we get home.'

Cathy looked at him and smiled. Even when they were in a relationship, he had taken on this role of medical advisor, despite her being equally qualified.

The rain had come on again after a brief respite. Chris nudged his windscreen wipers on and for a moment, the cemetery in front of them was sharp in focus and no longer blurred and distorted. The majority of the funeral-goers had parked on the road just along from where they now sat themselves. The headlights of the black car that had been beside the hearse within the churchyard suddenly came on. The white-yellow wavered and shook as the rain drummed across the glass.

'Must be the family,' he said unnecessarily as the car began to creep along the grey path towards the gates. The rest of the mourners stood aside, some stepping onto the grass to move well out of the way. The empty hearse followed.

Cathy sighed. 'The weather couldn't be more apt for a funeral really.'

They sat in silence, watching the crowds disperse. Some people were shaking hands, others hugging, before getting into cars. Cathy turned in her seat. 'Chris?'

He didn't look at her. His hands still rested on the steering wheel, but she saw his fingers tighten. 'Chris, you know I'm grateful. You know, all of this.' She made a sweeping gesture. 'I-I'm so grateful...'

He didn't speak.

'Chris?'

'You don't need to say any of this. You knew I'd help you.'

'You didn't have to. You could have shut the door in my face. You'd have every right to,' she said flopping back against the seat.

He snorted and she glanced sideways. 'I am sorry, about the way I left things,' she said. 'I shouldn't have... well, you know. You deserved an explanation and I didn't give you one. It must have been horrible. It all got too much for me. And then, one day led to another and then a week and I'd still not spoken to you...'

She didn't want to look at him but she heard him shifting in his seat. She shook her head sadly. 'It went on too long and then it became too hard to phone. I knew you were angry, but I didn't know how to call you.'

'How's Suzalinna?' he asked, clearing his throat.

'I've not spoken to her in a while either,' she admitted. 'I found out the week after we... well, we split. They were over the moon, both her and Saj when they found out she was expecting. You can imagine. And then, they were heading out to India. She was going to tell her parents while they were across. She'll not be able to fly soon.'

He nodded. 'I'm happy for them.'

'I am too,' she said. It was the truth, but it still hurt.

'Did you tell her?' he asked.

'About me? No. I thought about it. I might have, but I didn't want to spoil her big announcement. As soon as she said it, I knew I couldn't tell her. She'd constantly think she'd have to keep a check on her excitement out of loyalty to me. No. It was our secret. I kind of liked it being that way.' She glanced across at him but he looked away.

'We should get going now. They've just about gone.'

Cathy sighed and opened her door also, and stepped out into the rain.

'We weren't quite sure who to ask,' Cathy faltered. 'I hope you're able to help. It's just my aunt. I've been abroad and I didn't know her well, you see, but out of respect, I felt I should come. My mother, you see? She would have wanted it. It was only when I got back, just this last Monday, I heard the news and I assumed that my uncle would have chosen here.' Cathy dropped her voice. 'We don't talk these days after all that happened that Christmas. But I shouldn't bring it up...'

The minister looked slightly scandalised and nodded quickly as if he would rather do anything than hear about what her uncle had done during the festive period. 'You said that you don't know the date of the funeral?'

Cathy had no doubt so far that he believed her story, but why would he doubt such an innocent inquiry? 'No,' she said, 'I don't know the exact day, but you'd remember, I'm sure, because it was in the last few weeks. You can't have that many, can you? Unless they're dropping like flies.'

Cathy felt Chris's hand on her elbow. A signal to tone it down a bit perhaps. She blushed. It was surprising how easily the lies had come, but if she continued to over-elaborate, she might well end up tying herself in knots.

The minister coughed, a dry little bark. 'In the last few weeks?' he asked.

Cathy was sure that there had been a change, as if a flash of panic had crossed the man's face, but why? She felt her own heart quicken. They must surely be on the right track. The minister, though, couldn't be in on it.

They stood just inside the entrance to the church. Outside the rain continued to come down heavily. It thundered on the roof and Cathy wondered how the minister made himself heard during a service above the racket. Chris was by her side. She had told him to say little. Better that one of them take the lead, so as not to confuse the story.

'Yes. Perhaps two weeks ago,' Cathy went on, watching the man's face intently.

He was slightly stooped with a spine crumbled and warped by osteoarthritic change. His face had the thready redness that often comes with age, his cheeks looking flushed almost permanently. He still possessed a full head of hair. It had caught on the wind outside, though, and was grey and tousled.

'Influenza,' he said obscurely, and Cathy raised her eyebrows. 'This time of year, it's at its worst and we have had a number. What was the name?'

Cathy's heart was hammering in her throat and she knew she was blushing. She swallowed. 'It's complicated,' she said, looking sideways at Chris. 'I lost touch and I don't know what name she was going by. My uncle and her, you see? They were on and off and I wouldn't be surprised if it was a maiden name she'd returned to, but then again...'

'Well, the married or the maiden name would do,' the minister said doggedly.

Cathy was positive that the minister knew it was a lie. She felt that they were fencing around one another, testing to see who might break first. 'If you had a list or register, it would help,' she persisted.

'I'm afraid I don't have that,' he said. He smiled, but the creases of his mouth did not reach his eyes. 'Our sexton has all the documentation and so on. I'm afraid I've been of little help to your cause. Perhaps if you speak with your uncle.'

Cathy knew that this had been said with satisfaction. They thanked him for his time all the same and began to make their way to the car. They walked slowly, aware that the minister was watching them move across the cemetery.

'He knew,' Chris said quietly as they came in line with the path.

Cathy sighed. 'What did he have to hide though? We must be on the right track.' She shivered. 'This place gives me the creeps.' They walked past the grave that had just been occupied. The green cloth had been lifted in preparation for the small digger that had now appeared. 'What a job,' Cathy said, nodding to the empty cab.

'Sexton?' Chris asked. 'My great-uncle did it. Took real pride in his work too and it was only part-time. He was a postman the rest of the week.'

Cathy snorted. 'Still learning new things about you, Chris. I thought all of your family were doctors. But that is by far the most obscure bit of information you've ever revealed. Come on, let's get out of here. His eyes are burning into my back. I'll bet this is where they buried her.'

'He's been paid off to keep his mouth shut. That's my guess anyway,' Chris said as they got to the car. 'I wonder how else we could find out.'

They drove back to his house in silence. When they drew up outside, he turned off the engine and they sat in silence for some moments.

'I suppose we have to go to the police really,' he said finally. 'If someone's been murdered and then the body buried without the death being registered... It's pretty serious, Cathy.'

She looked out at the rain, following the drops that fell and gathered, tracking down the glass together, their combined weight bringing them far faster to their destination on the window ledge. She turned to him and smiled thinly. 'I'm scared, Chris. Really scared. I think something awful has happened and I think we're in real danger ourselves now.'

'But you're safe, Cathy. I don't understand. I'm with you and the police won't let anything happen to you.'

She nodded but didn't speak. But it wasn't that that frightened her; it was the truth that she feared the most. Of finding out that someone closer to her, even one of her colleagues, was involved in the deaths. It had been on her mind this last twenty-four hours. She had been avoiding it all along but the facts were there. She had thought that several times since this whole thing had started up. Her life had been put in danger. Not in as obvious a way as the last time when she was nearly run over but in more subtle ways. She wondered about her faintness at the gym and about Dr Kidd holding a syringe in his hand and suggesting he give her something to help her heart rate.

That was one thing, though, but even more frightening was the suggestion that the criminal had been far closer to home. The medical records for Mr and Mrs Steer had been deleted from their computers. Had the culprit been within their practice building? Had it been one of the GPs themselves? Cathy recalled Euan's odd behaviour. His sudden disappearance on the pretext of going back to Ireland for a funeral. Had he been there or had he instead been arranging the disappearance of two of their patients? He had been on call that night, after all. She thought of his insistence that she looked unwell herself, that she should get him to check her bloods. Had he been trying to inject her with something also but hadn't been able as she had asked James to do the favour instead?

'Come on,' Chris said, breaking into her thoughts. 'Let's go in and I'll make you something to eat. You look exhausted again. I'll give you more of those painkillers too.'

Cathy looked again at him. She had noticed as she got into his car that the rear tail light was flickering. She felt a weary sense that something dreadful was about to happen.

29

She hadn't seen the car parked opposite the house until they were at the door. Chris was messing about with the keys and she looked sadly over the road and noticed it then. There were two men inside the dark saloon and both were doing everything they could to look inconspicuous.

'Chris,' she hissed. 'Hurry up.'

By now, she didn't know who she could trust. Was it the eastern Europeans back again, this time to forcibly get the truth about Mrs Steer from her? Chris dropped the keys and cursed. How could she have been so stupid? He was in on it too, of course. He had led them to her. Cathy looked again across at the car. The two men were now getting out. They both wore suits and looked official.

'Jesus,' she said and then, without thought, she leapt from the top step, landing at the bottom with a grunt. The pain in her ankle was excruciating, but she knew it was now or never. She got to the gate before them and swung it back, letting it clang loudly against the wall. She heard Chris's voice, quiet at first and then he was shouting after her. Calling her name again and again.

'Cathy,' he kept calling. 'Cathy, wait!'

The road was downhill and she slid and splashed as she picked up speed, twisting this way and that, looking for a way out. Behind her, she heard the thumping of footsteps. She squealed in panic. Oh God, what was she going to do now? Her ankle was making her too slow. She heard the steps behind her nearing and then the breath of a man, catching in gasps.

'No!' she screamed. In desperation, she swung around and faced him. Her eyes were wide and she was panting in terror. She raised her arms to protect herself. But he was holding a syringe. It was over.

She had been here before. In this very room. Nothing had changed. The chairs were just as low and itchy on her legs, the windows were as grand, and rattled in the wind. The psychiatrist had gone. He had been sympathetic and had listened but she knew he didn't believe her. She wondered why she bothered at all. No one wanted to hear about the Steers. They all thought she was mad.

She had been given a mild sedative. It was the only way they could get her in the car. Her body felt less tight but her mind was still full of restless ideas and racing thoughts. Since arriving, she had been handed an antipsychotic tablet. It was the one she should have been taking regularly but had not. She swallowed it without question. There was no choice. She didn't want to be like this. It was just how it had turned out. She tried to explain it all to the psychiatrist. He had nodded and smiled but his eyes had remained serious.

'It might take a week or so. Maybe not even that,' he had said. 'Stay here, for the time being, Dr Moreland. I'm not sectioning you. Please don't make me. I'm offering you a safe bed, just to rest up until you're fit to go home. Your colleagues have been terribly concerned about you after you absconded from the hospital. No one knew where you were.'

They had allowed her one visitor on the condition that she wasn't to speak with him alone. By the door, the male psychiatric nurse sat impassive, doing his utmost to be discreet, but an ever-felt presence all the same.

'How could you?' she spat at him.

Chris shook his head. He was seated opposite her. His left knee bobbed and she was reminded of her encounter with Archie Steer and the faded sole of his otherwise immaculate shoes. 'You've got to believe me, Cathy. I had no idea,' Chris said.

She sniffed in revulsion. 'How did they find me then?'

He didn't meet her eyes. He could barely bring himself to look at her. She stared mercilessly at him, unblinking, daring him to deny it.

He sighed. 'The other night,' he said. 'When you had fallen asleep, I went back to your house. Oh, Cathy, don't. I know it was wrong. I took the keys from your rucksack.' He glanced up, his face was full of anxious appeal. 'But, Cathy, they had your best interests at heart, just like me. People have been worried about your health. I think they had been hoping to talk with you at home, to agree a time for you to come in and speak to the psychiatrists.'

'Why were you at my house?' she asked, but she knew the answer as soon as she asked. 'It was the tablets, wasn't it?'

He nodded.

'You had no bloody right! I told you the house was dangerous to go back to. Another couple of days off the antipsychotics wouldn't have changed a thing. How could you? Trying to control me, just like the rest of them.' She shot a look at the psychiatric nurse who was studying his hands. 'He's probably one of the Russian spies, you know? Perfect cover, working here, of course.' She grimaced at the nurse. 'Looking for Mrs Steer?' she sneered. 'You'll not find her here. She dead!'

The man shifted in his seat but made no eye contact.

'Cathy, please stop this,' Chris begged. 'Listen, I was worried. No, I'll be honest. I was terrified for you. I've never seen you so jumpy and agitated. I've been watching you since you arrived on my doorstep, afraid of what you might do to yourself. Your ankle should have been rested and those scrapes on your arms and legs... One of them is really deep, I've seen it. You should have had a tetanus jab. Your weight too. You're skin and bones. God knows what you've done to yourself.'

Cathy looked at him in disgust. 'And you expect me to believe you didn't call psychiatry?'

'No, I did not,' he said, sounding angry now. 'I should have done. I'm a plastic surgeon, for God's sake, not a counsellor. I don't know what to say to you. I do know you needed your antipsychotics, though.'

'I told you a day didn't matter. I'd not be surprised if you've been talking to James and Euan about me too. Did you get their numbers from my phone? Did you ring them up and chat my case through with them too?'

He shook his head. 'I don't know what to say to make you believe me. What I've said is the truth. I admit I did the wrong thing going to your house last night, but I wanted the tablets for you. It was done with the best intentions. You needed to come in here. It was the right thing really, it just happened in the wrong way. You'd never have agreed to come of your own accord though, let's face it. I thought if I could somehow get you to take the tablets...'

'Have you given one to me already, without my knowledge?' she asked suddenly.

He looked incredulous. 'No, Cathy. I wouldn't do that.'

She shrugged. 'I wouldn't put it past you. I wouldn't put

anything past you now. I don't know what to believe. I noticed your car by the way,' she said, smiling nastily. 'You thought I'd not realised, but I'm no fool.'

He looked confused.

'I thought it was Dr Kidd,' she went on, shaking her head. 'By coincidence, his rear light is faulty too. You've been following me these last two weeks, maybe longer. Don't deny it. I know it all. Even Suzalinna's trip back to India. She was in on it too!'

His head was in his hands and he didn't speak.

'I knew it,' she said triumphantly. 'Well, what is your involvement in the Steer's disappearances? I never did believe it when you told me you were in Australia working. All that nonsense about coming back to Glainkirk because you were homesick was a cover. What are you then? Some kind of a spy for a drug company? Your job was to trail me, wasn't it? You were told to do everything in your power to keep me from finding out the truth.' Cathy shook her head in revulsion. 'And what did I do, but play right into your hands? My God, you must have laughed when I turned up on your doorstep begging for help. You must have thought all of your Christmases had come at once. What a bloody fool I was.'

He looked up and his face was full of despair. 'Cathy,' he said. 'If you could just hear yourself. Please, darling...'

'Don't darling me. You lost that right a long time ago. Traitor. Judas. God knows how you can sleep at night.'

The nurse by the door shuffled his feet.

'Please, Cathy,' he said again. 'Don't do this.'

But she couldn't hear him anymore. She turned from him and then as he went to touch her knee, she spat in his face. The nurse got up and pointed to the door. Chris rose slowly from his chair, wiping his cheek.

'Cathy, I'm sorry,' he said softly. 'As you're getting better, I hope you'll realise...'

But his words were wasted.

Over the coming days though, she dwelt on what he had said a good deal. Her psychiatrist was infinitely patient with her. He listened to her rambling story again and again. Sometimes at night, as she lay in the narrow hospital bed watching the shadows of nurses pausing at her door and then passing by, she whispered to herself, trying to make sense of it all. Why had they taken the Steers? How had it come to be that they had been murdered and buried in a legitimate graveyard but with no documentation? Why had the floors of the lodge house smelled of disinfectant? Who had posed as a doctor in the first place, and given the name of her dead GP partner? Had it been Chris or Dr Kidd who had been following her, and why? Who were the eastern Europeans and what was it that Mrs Steer had that they wanted so badly? Had they been trying to kill her also? Why had everyone at the practice been so anxious to check her own bloods? What had Mr Steer done to disgrace the family pharmaceutical business, and why had he been ostracised by his own brothers? Finally, what about the third generation? Had Marjorie Steer been pregnant? Had that been why she was taken and killed?

Cathy slept on and off, even during the day occasionally, as the nights in the hospital were all but impossible. They woke her at mealtimes and didn't force-feed her, but sat doggedly by her side until the plate was clean. Gradually, perhaps on the fourth day, although she wasn't quite sure herself, she was deemed well enough to have visitors again. James, her weary senior partner came, accompanied again by Chris. Both looked haggard. They said that they felt they had let her down. She shook her head, the strands of hair, freshly washed that morning, falling across her face.

Before they left, Cathy appealed to James. It had been bothering her acutely and she felt a fool for having not looked into it already. Now that she was in the hospital though with no computer access, she was powerless to find out. James didn't look happy, but he agreed to do it at last and promised to return the following day with the answer to her question. The housekeeper's red hands, the hurried burial... It all seemed to point in one direction. It had actually been Chris's overprotective comment about her not looking after herself properly, that had put the idea first in her head. Over the past few days, it had gradually begun to fall into place. Perhaps it was the antipsychotics kicking in, she would never really know.

When James returned the following day, his face was grim.

'I've brought another visitor, Cathy,' he said. 'I wanted to check with you first before he came in.'

Cathy looked to the door. James had closed it behind him as he came in, but there was a glass panel in the top.

'It can't be,' she said. She looked at James in confusion. 'So, I was right then?'

James nodded and beckoned for Mr Adam Steer to come into the room.

30

'Your wife?' she asked immediately, but Mr Steer shook his head. 'I'm so sorry,' she told him. She paused out of respect but there were so many questions that needed to be answered.

'Where did they take you?' she asked finally, looking down at her hands that were clasped tightly in her lap. 'It must have been a private hospital. I've been going out of my mind trying to work it out.'

James and Mr Steer sat before her. Mr Steer had lost a considerable amount of weight. His once strong physique had withered, which seemed quite impossible given that it had only been fourteen days since Cathy had last seen him, but then, he had been fighting for his life all that time.

'I don't know why it didn't click,' Cathy said, shaking her head. 'The India trip should have given it away I suppose, but then I didn't know the company had been involved. When I was outside the family house and overheard your brothers mentioning a third generation, I assumed it was something to do with a child. I wondered if your wife had been pregnant and if it had implications on the business. Would the child inherit some of the fortune? Silly. Of course, they were talking about third generation vaccine production,' she said, shaking her head ruefully. 'It was that, wasn't it? God knows how I could have been so slow. But I still don't understand how your wife...?'

'She was in the lab out in India. I had no idea she had come into contact with it, obviously.' His voice sounded weak and he cleared his throat. It made a rasping sound and he looked as if he was about to cough, but instead, his eyes filled with tears.

Cathy didn't know if it was with the effort of not coughing, or with emotion. Granted, the marriage had clearly been in trouble, but to lose your wife in such a manner seemed unspeakable.

'But surely there must have been high security,' she persisted. 'How did she get hold of the live virus? I thought she was a photographer by trade, not a scientist. She shouldn't have been involved in it at all.'

Mr Steer sighed. 'Marjorie was a medical photographer.'

'Ah...' Cathy shook her head. She had been so stupid this whole time.

'She'd never been part of the business at all but I think you know we'd been having some marital issues.' Mr Steer shrugged his hollow shoulders. 'She felt pushed out, I suppose. My family aren't the easiest. I persuaded Eddie, my oldest brother, to employ her as a campaign and publicity photographer. The US government had wanted the positive promotion if things kicked off. It was intended to act as a deterrent to any splinter groups. They knew that the live virus was capable of being cultured with enough money behind it. The key was to have plenty of the vaccine ready and waiting. Obviously, the hope was that it would never be needed for max immunisations but they had to be prepared. Marjorie wasn't meant to be anywhere near the high security part of the lab. Mainly she was doing shots of the lab technicians at work and the vials of newly produced vaccine.

God knows how she came into contact with the live virus. I can only assume that she was trying to be clever with her pictures. The laboratory went into lock down as soon as they heard there had been a breach.'

'She showed no symptoms on the plane coming home though? I presume it would have been far more serious if she had. It was only back on UK soil that her throat ached? The rest of the people on the flight then...?'

'None affected, thank God. They have all been checked discreetly.'

'But you?'

'Yes, but only a very minor strain and no skin involvement at all. I was kept in isolation as a precaution.'

'And me?' Cathy asked.

Mr Steer looked at James who nodded.

'A lesser strain, possibly, if anything at all. You had antiviral treatment as soon as you came in here along with the vaccine and you weren't contagious at any point. Smallpox can affect people in different ways, as I'm sure you know. You were lucky. If you did have it, it was the minor version.'

'You knew?' she asked James. 'Was that why you and Euan wanted to do my bloods? Dr Kidd, did he know too?'

James looked embarrassed. 'Cathy, the truth is that none of us knew. We wanted to check your bloods because we were genuinely concerned about you. You've run yourself into the ground and recently, you've looked so pale. None of us could have possibly suspected it was smallpox. I thought it had been completely eradicated years ago. None of us knew about the virus at all.'

'It should have been eliminated long ago. It had been,' Mr Steer said. 'My father's company had been requested last year to begin this vaccine development programme. Of course, there was already an inoculation available but with the suggestion of new mutations possibly being developed elsewhere... Well, we had to do something. Apparently, there had been some intelligence suggesting that an extremist terrorist cell was attempting to recreate the virus again from the corpses of exhumed victims. The disease was eliminated in the 1970s. There are three vials of the active disease still kept in high-security institutes. One is in India, and two in America. Our pharmaceutical company was chosen because of our involvement already in developing the influenza vaccines. No one could have realised how this might end.'

'It explains why your brother, Archie, was so hostile. My God, he seemed angry with you, but of course, it wasn't your doing,' Cathy said.

'He was furious when the lab called ahead and warned him about a possible breach in security just before Marjorie flew home.'

'And of course, he had come down to your lodge house to ask how you both were, knowing full-well that your wife had possibly been accidentally exposed to the virus. But why not tell you what had happened? Why not explain what was really wrong with Marjorie?'

Mr Steer looked at the ground. 'He assumed I was the one who had breached security. My brother thought I was trying to do some backhanded deal with another company and I had accidentally infected my wife in the process...'

Cathy nodded. 'And I assume that he didn't call the out-of-hours doctors at all when you came running up to the house that night?'

'I'll never forgive him,' Mr Steer said. 'He's since told me that he was instructed to get her out to a contained environment. They took her to the private hospital, but she died within an hour. There was nothing they could do. It was quick. That's a great comfort to me.'

'And you?'

'They came back for me the next day, cleared the house out to make sure too.'

'I should have realised when I smelled the bleach. The sole of your brother's shoe was faded too showing he'd been there when the disinfectant was damp, and then there was the housekeeper...?'

'Mrs Sturrock?'

'Yes, I saw her hands were red when she opened the door. I thought it was contact dermatitis and I was probably right if she'd been involved in the clean-up operation.'

Mr Steer nodded.

'So, they took you to be isolated and treated, and yet, the family feud continues?'

'That's a long-term thing, to be fair,' Mr Steer said. 'It was always difficult to know quite how we fitted into my father's plans, growing up. He wanted one of us to take on the pharmaceutical business. Archie and Eddie went travelling after university. I stayed at home. While they were away living the high life, my father asked me to come on board. I don't think they ever forgave me. They thought I'd muscled in, that I'd planned the whole thing. At first, it seemed like I'd struck gold when Dad gave me the reins, but it wasn't so easy, and when my brothers returned and found I was already on Dad's board of directors, they obviously weren't best pleased.' He sighed. 'To cut a long story short, I wasn't any good at it,' he continued. 'Eddie was by far the most business-minded of the three of us. I made a few mistakes along the way and bowed out, perhaps not as gracefully as I should have. I was still involved obviously, but not on the managerial side. It was still a job, and by then I'd run up a shedload of debts. When Dad killed himself, the business was in a pretty dismal state. Archie blamed me. The US vaccine deal was meant to make us rich again. I think they thought that if they sent me out to India to oversee things, it would get me out of the way at least for a bit. Then I made a pig's ear of that too...'

'Oh dear...' Cathy said. 'And things were bad enough that when you returned you were living in the lodge rather than the big house?'

'Oh, that was for Marjorie. She hated my brothers and they hated her. It was the only way she said she'd come back.'

'And I thought she'd come home to take up with another man. For a long time, I thought the same as the police when you went to them that first night: that she'd run off and left you, but you were too arrogant to admit it. I'm sorry,' she said.

Mr Steer shook his head and smiled. 'India had done us both good. Things were a lot better. I think living a simpler life suited us both well and we found again what was important for us. She had been having an affair with a local man before we left. I never knew who it was. It was very much in the past. We'd returned and were keen to make a fresh start.'

'I'm sorry,' Cathy repeated. 'It doesn't seem fair. I assume that this can't go public? So, she couldn't ever have had a funeral as such.'

'No. No one can know anything about it. I know where she's buried and I'll visit the grave to pay my respects but for security reasons, the grave will remain unmarked.'

Cathy nodded. 'Did you know that your medical notes, along with your wife's, were deleted off the computers at work? You essentially no longer exist.'

'It was a precaution, so Eddie said. It couldn't get out.' Mr Steer sighed. 'I've had a good chance to think about things and I don't know that Scotland has much to offer me now anyway. I may travel to the US and eventually take on a supervisory role in one of our labs over there, at least until I feel more like myself again. Staying here would feel wrong now. Too many memories.'

Cathy nodded. She turned to James who had so far sat in

silence. 'James, I have to ask. Does Euan know anything about this?'

'No. He doesn't need to. It will have to remain our secret, Cathy,' he said. 'It's a pity you can't tell anyone. Having survived smallpox would carry some kudos, I suppose.'

Even Mr Steer, despite his grief, managed to raise a smile.

Cathy stayed on a further five days at the psychiatric hospital. Chris came to collect her first thing in the morning.

'I've brought someone else,' he said coming into the side room and shifting her overnight bag on the bed so the other visitor could sit down.

Cathy went to her friend and they held one another for a long time. Then Cathy pushed her back so that she could look her up and down. 'No bump yet?' she asked. Suzalinna shook her head.

'Not yet, silly. I'm only sixteen weeks.' There was a pause and neither of them seemed to know what to say. 'I'm so sorry we lost touch,' Suzalinna said. 'I don't know how it happened. I had no idea you'd been unwell again. I've been so caught up with work and going back to see my parents, and this,' she said, looking down at herself.

Cathy grinned. 'When can we start buying things? You're not going to be all superstitious, are you? I can't wait to be an honorary auntie.'

31

'Do we have to sign some secrecy contract or something?' Cathy asked Chris later that afternoon.

She was in his kitchen and the kettle had just boiled. Chris, who had been pulling a load of clean washing from the machine, snorted.

'Idiot,' he said and threw a damp sock at her head.

'I suppose a good few of us know though if you think about it,' she said, retrieving the sock and lobbing it back into the basket. 'There's me, you and James. Then there's the entire Steer family. My goodness, they must have been frantic with worry, trying to cover the whole mess up. Going as far as to delete patient records. I assume that was Eddie, the oldest brother, in person. He had the audacity to walk into our practice and to tamper with the files. Unbelievable really, but the girls didn't even question him. The family were desperate to obliterate any trace of Adam and Marjorie both within the lodge house and on file. God knows what they planned to say if Marjorie pulled through. What a mess. No wonder the brothers were rude to me. They must have been beside themselves when I started digging around and asking questions.'

'I still don't understand though. What happened that night when Mr Steer found his wife unwell? Did he call the GPs or not, and who was the person posing as a doctor if he did?'

Cathy laughed bitterly. 'It was something you said in the cemetery that put me onto that, as it happens. Do you remember telling me about one of your great uncles working as a sexton?'

Chris looked confused.

'No, it was just that you said he had done two jobs. Both a sexton and something else.'

'A postman,' Chris laughed.

'Whatever,' she said. 'Well, it made me think a bit. I puzzled a good deal about the phoney GP. Mr Steer had gone up to the mansion house and had asked his brother Archie to phone because his own mobile had mysteriously gone missing.'

'Stolen by Archie earlier when he'd been down to enquire after his sister-in-law?'

'Yes. Well, of course, the last thing Archie was going to do was to ring up the out-of-hours doctors. He'd already been told by someone high up that the situation was as grave as it could be and no one could know.

'He had a local man already employed as a bit of a skivvy for the family. He'd done a bit of taxiing here and there for them, a few odd jobs when they'd needed. The man had been short on cash himself and although he had no medical training, he had been exposed to the way doctors worked. It was a bit of a gift for Archie and Eddie Steer when they realised how useful he could be to them.' She paused and smiled. 'Still no idea?' she asked, and he shrugged. 'It was one of the out-of-hours drivers, as it happens. A man named Dave. It took me a while to work it out too, although I really should have realised sooner. He was even reading a novel on a fictional pandemic when I last saw him.'

Cathy shook her head in annoyance. 'No, I was very slow and stupid. What, I suspect, was Archie or Eddie had probably been waiting in the car when he went inside the lodge house to do his little doctor impersonation. They primed him with what he had to say and that he was to get Mrs Steer out of the house no matter what. They had to get her to a safe place to be isolated. It was a risk telling someone else. Perhaps they didn't even explain the whole story to him, just paid him handsomely to keep his mouth shut and to play the game.'

'What if he caught it too?'

'I guess he was classed as disposable. Horrible really. He could have been offered the vaccine I suppose, but they were probably short on time by that point. I have no doubt that Eddie and Archie were fully vaccinated as soon as the concern was raised, as were all of the laboratory workers.'

'But not their younger brother?'

Cathy shook her head. 'Sadly no. Mr Steer wasn't meant to be at any risk though if only his wife hadn't been in the labs nosing around. He was dealing with the business, not the chemical research.'

'It was a big risk involving someone like Dave,' Chris said.

'It was. It still is. Too many people know really.'

'And the eastern European man? I'll admit, I did wonder if it was a delusion of yours when you became unwell.'

Cathy nodded. 'No, he was real enough. I've spoken to the police about that already and they're looking into it. I didn't want to talk about it in front of Mr Steer. His wife of course wasn't simply having a poke around the labs taking photographs. Only a fool would believe that. No, Mrs Steer had been playing a very dangerous game indeed. Remember, the whole reason Traxium was beginning mass production of the third-generation vaccine was because of intelligence on a potential terrorist cell? I believe Mrs Steer had somehow been employed to remove a sample of the live virus. I've read about clever scientists managing to mutate an already deadly virus to make it resistant to a vaccine. Perhaps that was what they planned to do.'

'But she didn't manage to remove any of the live virus, did she?'

'Only on herself,' Cathy said sadly. 'I suppose even that might have been useful to them.'

'My God,' Chris said with feeling. 'If news got out...'

Cathy shrugged. 'It would cause mass hysteria if people knew that there had been a case of smallpox in Britain after it had been declared eradicated some fifty years ago.' She sighed, thinking of Mrs Steer and the almost catastrophic error of judgement the woman had made. It had cost her her life but it might so easily have cost many more.

Chris had straightened up from his washing basket. 'You're not getting maudlin again, are you? Self-pity didn't take long to kick in.' He smiled at her. 'I know you're probably thinking about work. You're established on the right dose now and Euan will be keeping an eye on you when you go back. He'll need you back soon though if you're to sort out James's replacement.'

'I spoke to James about that, as it happens. It seems Euan might have a solution.'

'Not Linda, surely?' Chris asked. Even he had been told about the infamous salaried GP.

Cathy shook her head and grinned. 'No, although to be fair, once again, she's not let the side down while I've been away. It's funny, but I did start to wonder if she had been somehow involved in the whole conspiracy when I heard her husband worked for the same pharmaceutical company as the Steers. I was getting a bit paranoid by then though, and perhaps I wasn't thinking straight.' She glanced sideways at Chris and he smirked. 'No, but Euan's idea apparently came to him, while he was back in Dublin at his grandmother's funeral. He said he was networking a bit and got talking to one of his trainers. The man's an older GP and is looking to move over to Scotland in the new year as he has a postgraduate university lecturer offer. He needs to keep his hand in with clinical stuff though and was hoping to pick up at least three full days as a partner. It's not as many hours as we wanted, but we'd then be free to offer Linda a few extra sessions to keep her sweet. If it worked out...'

'Well, it sounds ideal,' Chris said. 'I worry about you taking on too much, and I'd be glad to know there was someone else.'

'I've still got Stuart looking out for me,' she said.

'Dr Kidd? Yes. There's that also. You never did explain to me how he fitted into the whole Steer saga.'

Cathy sighed. 'It's rather sad,' she said. 'He really did love Mrs Steer. I think they had been planning to set up a home together. I don't know how the thing started. Maybe they met at the gym. Oh, I know what her husband said, that they had patched things up when they were out in India and that the marriage was back on track. Maybe Mr Steer needed to believe that himself to get over it. But remember also what the police thought that very first night Mr Steer went missing? They looked in her diary. She had been writing in it just that evening before she became unwell. She had fallen out of love with her husband and it was Stuart she had come home for, although she didn't mention him by name. I puzzled over who the potential lover might be for some time. The car following me was a hint. That, and the footprint in the flower border. When I considered the evidence of him taking on extra shifts and behaving so out of character, it did all seem to make sense. His own marriage was failing, he was trailing up and down Ancrum Road. Now we know why. He had to be the missing link. He was Marjorie's lover. I think he was as desperate as I was to find out the truth.'

'Does he know now?'

'Not about the smallpox, no, but he knows that she died of course. They said it was a pulmonary embolus from having been on the flight. It's not so uncommon. He was devastated, so James said. I think he'd been working every hour he could to claw in enough capital for them to start over together.'

'He had a family though. Three kids?'

'Love does make you do silly things though,' Cathy sighed, and then blushing, she looked down at her hands. 'So, Chris. How does our story end?'

His face was serious and she thought for a moment, she had been too direct. He had already said she should stay until she was feeling more like herself but maybe she had misjudged things.

'Well, you've already accused me of being a murderer,' he said. 'I suppose things can only go up from here.'

A smile pricked at her lips and she nodded. Yes. Things could only improve now.

THE END

ACKNOWLEDGEMENTS

Many thanks to the Bloodhound team for believing in the series. Landing Clare as an editor was an absolute gift and I am forever grateful to have worked with her on all seven books.

Thanks especially to my husband for repeatedly reminding me when times were tough and ideas didn't come, that I was safe and loved whatever happened with Dr Cathy. I know he put up with some ribbing at work when people heard I was writing a doctor series but dealt with it all in good humour as always.

To my parents, I thank you for your encouragement and curiosity. A good deal of my bookish interest comes from growing up so thank you for introducing me to Enid Blyton so early on!

Finally, thank you to my readers for taking Dr Cathy Moreland to their hearts. She saw me through some very dark days when my own bipolar was uncontrolled and I hope she goes on to inspire others struggling just to get through the day.

A NOTE FROM THE PUBLISHER

Thank you for reading this book. If you enjoyed it please do consider leaving a review on Amazon to help others find it too.

We hate typos. All of our books have been rigorously edited and proofread, but sometimes mistakes do slip through. If you have spotted a typo, please do let us know and we can get it amended within hours.

info@bloodhoundbooks.com